ISOBARS

Fiction by the same author

The Ivory Swing
The Tiger in the Tiger Pit
Borderline
Dislocations (short stories)
Charades

ISOBARS

stories by

JANETTE TURNER HOSPITAL

M&S

Canadian Cataloguing in Publication Data

Hospital, Janette Turner, 1942–
    Isobars

Canadian ed.
ISBN 0–7710–4223–X

I. Title.

PS8565.055417 1991   C813'.54   C91–093085–6
PR9199.3.H67I7 1991

First published 1990 by University of Queensland Press,
Box 42, St. Lucia, Queensland, 4067, Australia

Printed and bound in Canada

McClelland & Stewart Inc.
The Canadian Publishers
481 University Avenue
Toronto, Ontario M5G 2E9

Acknowledgements

These stories, sometimes under different titles and in slightly different form, have appeared in the following magazines:
Australia: *Meanjin, Scripsi, Overland, The Australian, Imago, Fine Line, LinQ*, and *Southerly*. Also in *Expressway*, ed. Helen Daniel (Penguin, 1989) and *The Australian Bedside Book*, ed. Geoffrey Dutton (Macmillan, 1987).
Canada: *Room of One's Own, Descant, Chatelaine*.
U.S.A.: *Translation* (Columbia University), *Prairie Schooner*.
U.K.: "The Loss of Faith" in the anthology *Best Short Stories* (1990), edited by Giles Gordon and David Hughes (Heinemann).

"The Mango Tree" (under the title "After Long Absence"), "Morgan Morgan," "The Bloody Past, The Wandering Future," previously appeared in the Australian (University of Queensland Press) and U.S. (Louisiana State University Press) editions of Janette Turner Hospital's first short story collection, *Dislocations*.

The poem "Come-by-Chance" by A.B. (Banjo) Paterson is from *Song of the Pen: Complete Works 1901–1941* (Sydney: Lansdowne Press, 1983), by permission of Rosamund Campbell and Philippa Harvie.

Contents

The Mango Tree

For years it has branched extravagantly in dreams, but the mango tree outside the kitchen window in Brisbane is even greener than the jubilant greens of memory. I could almost believe my mother has been out there with spit and polish, buffing up each leaf for my visit. I suggest this to her and she laughs, handing me a china plate.

Her hands are a bright slippery pink from the soap suds and the fierce water, and when I take the plate it is as though I have touched the livid element of a stove. In the nick of time, I grunt something unintelligible in lieu of swearing. "Oh heck," I mumble, cradling the plate and my seared fingers in the tea-towel. "I'd forgotten." And we both laugh. It is one of those family idiosyncrasies, an heirloom of sorts, passed down with the plate itself which entered family history on my grandmother's wedding day. The women in my mother's family have always believed that dishwashing water should be just on the leeside of boiling, and somehow, through sheer conviction that cleanliness is next to godliness, I suppose, their hands can calmly swim in it.

I glance at the wall above the refrigerator, and yes, the needlepoint text is still there, paler from another decade of sun, but otherwise undiminished: *He shall try you in a refiner's fire.*

"Do you still have your pieces?" my mother asks.

She means the cup, saucer, and plate from my grand-mother's dinner set, which is of fine bone china, but Victorian, out of fashion. The heavy band of black and pale orange and gold leaf speaks of boundaries that can-not be questioned.

"I'd never part with it," I say.

And I realise from the way in which she smiles and closes her eyes that she has been afraid it would be one more thing I would have jettisoned. I suppose it seems rather arbitrary to my parents, what I have rejected and what I have hung on to. My mother is suspended there, dishmop in hand, eyes closed, for several seconds. She is "giving thanks". I think with irritation: nothing has ever been secular in this house. Not even the tiniest thing.

"Leave this," my mother says, before I am halfway through the sensation of annoyance. "I'll finish. You sit outside and get some writing done."

And I think helplessly: It's always been like this, a seesaw of frustration and tenderness. Whose childhood and adolescence could have been more stifled or more pampered?

"But I *like* doing this with you," I assure her. "I really do." She smiles and "gives thanks" again, a fleeting and exasperating and totally unconscious gesture. "Hon-estly," I add, precisely because it has suddenly become untrue, because my irritation has surged as quixotically as the Brisbane River in flood. "It's one of . . ." but I decide not to add that it is one of the few things we can do in absolute harmony.

"You should enjoy the sun while you can," she says. Meaning: before you go back to those unimaginable Canadian winters. "Besides, you'll want to write your letters." She pauses awkwardly, delicately avoiding the inexplicable fact that the others have not yet arrived. She cannot imagine a circumstance that would have taken her away, even temporarily, from her husband and children. All her instincts tell her that such action is negligent and immoral. But she will make no judgements, regardless of inner cost. "And then," she says valiantly, "there's your book. You shouldn't be wasting time. . . . You should get on with your book." My book, which they fear will embarrass them again. My book, which will cause them such pride and bewilderment and sorrow. "Off with you," she says. "Sun's waiting."

I've been back less than twenty-four hours and already I'm dizzy — the same old roller-coaster of anger and love. I surrender the damp linen tea-towel which is stamped with the coats of arms of all the Australian states. I gather up notepad and pen, and head for the sun.

They are old comforters, the sun and the mango tree. I think I've always been pagan at heart, a sun worshipper, perhaps all Queensland children are. There was always far more solace in the upper branches of this tree than in the obligatory family Bible reading and prayers that followed dinner. I wrap my arms around the trunk, I press my cheek to the rough bark, remembering that wasteland of time, the fifth grade.

I can smell it again, sharp and bitter, see all the cruel young faces. The tree sap still stinks of it. My fingers touch scars in the trunk, the blisters of nail heads hammered in long years ago when we read somewhere that the iron improved the mangoes. The rust comes off now on my hands, a dark stain. I am falling down the endless concrete stairs, I feel the pushing again, the kicking, blood coming from somewhere, I can taste that old fear.

I reach for the branch where I hid; lower now, it seems — which disturbs me. Not as inaccessibly safe as I had thought.

Each night, the pale face of my brother would float from behind the glass of his isolation ward and rise through the mango leaves like a moon. I never asked, I was afraid to ask, "Will he die?" And the next day at school, and the next, I remember, remember: all the eyes pressed up against my life, staring, mocking, hostile, menacing.

There was a mark on me.

I try now to imagine myself as one of the others. I suppose I would simply have seen what they saw: someone dipped in death, someone trailing a shadowy cloak of contamination, someone wilfully dangerous. Why should I blame them that they had to ward me off?

This had, in any case, been foretold.

I had known we were strange from my earliest weeks in the first grade. "The nurse has arrived with your needles," our teacher said, and everyone seemed to know what she was talking about. "You'll go when your name is called. It doesn't hurt."

"It does so," called out Patrick Murphy, and was made to stand in the corner.

"With a name like that," said the teacher, "I'm not surprised."

She was busy unfurling and smoothing out the flutter of consent letters which we had all dutifully returned from home, some of us arriving with the letters safety-pinned to our pinafores. The teacher singled out one of the slips, her brow furrowed.

"I see we have our share of religious fanatics," she said. She began to prowl between the desks, waving the white letter like a flag. "Someone in our class," she announced, "is a killer." She stopped beside my desk and I could smell her anger, musky and acrid and damp. It was something I recognised, having smelled it when our cat was playing with a bird, though I could not have said what part of the smell came from which creature. The teacher put her finger on my shoulder, a summons, and I followed to the front of the class. "This person," said the teacher, "is our killer."

And everyone, myself included, solemnly observed. I looked at my hands and feet, curious. A killer, I thought, tasting the double *l* with interest and terror, my tongue forward against the roof of my mouth.

"Irresponsible! Morally irresponsible!" The teacher's voice was like that of our own pastor when he climbed into the pulpit. She was red in the face. I waited for her, my first victim, to go up in smoke. "Ignorant fanatics," she said, "you and your family. You're the kind who cause an epidemic."

I always remembered the word, not knowing what it meant. I saw it as dark and cumulous, freighted with classroom awe, a bringer of lightning bolts. *Epidemic*. I sometimes credit that moment with the birth of my passionate interest in the pure sound of arrangements of syllables. *Epidemic*. And later, of course, in the fifth grade, *diphtheria*, a beautiful word, but deadly.

I know a lot about words, about their sensuous surfaces, the way the tongue licks at them. And about the depth charges they carry.

My mother brings tea and an Arnott's biscuit, though I have been out here scarcely an hour, and though I have not written a word. I have been sitting here crushing her ferns, my back against the mango tree, remembering Patrick Murphy: how no amount of standings-in-the-corner or of canings (I can hear the surf-like whisper of the switch against his bare calves) could put a dent in his exuberance or his self-destructive honesty.

Once, in the first grade, he retrieved my shoes from the railway tracks where Jimmy Simpson had placed them. In the fifth grade he was sometimes able to protect me, and word reached me that one of his black eyes was on my account. One day I brought him home, and my parents said later they had always believed that some Catholics would be saved, that some were among the Lord's Anointed in spite of rank superstition and the idols in their churches. But I was not seriously encouraged to hope that Patrick Murphy would be in the company of this elect. When my mother offered him homemade lemonade, he told her it beat the bejesus out of the stuff you could get at the shops. He also said that most of the kids at school were full of ratshit and that only one or two sheilas made the place any better than buggery.

One morning Patrick Murphy and I woke up and it was time for high school. We went to different ones, and lost touch, though I saw him one Friday night in the heart of Brisbane, on the corner of Adelaide and Albert Streets, outside the Commonwealth Bank. The Tivoli and the Wintergarden ("dens of iniquity," the pastor said) were emptying and he was part of that crowd, his brushback flopping into his eyes, a girl on his arm. The girl was stunning in a sleazy kind of way: close-fitting slacks and spike heels, a tight sweater, platinum blonde hair and crimson lips. My kind of sheila, I imagined Patrick Murphy grinning, and the thought of his mouth on hers disturbed me. I rather imagined that an extra dollop of original sin came with breasts like hers. I rather hoped so.

I was praying Patrick Murphy wouldn't see me.

From my very reluctant spot in the circle, I could see that his eyes were wholly on his girl's cleavage. I moved slightly, so that my back was to the footpath, but so that I could still see him from out of the corner of my eye. Our circle, which took up two parking spaces, was bisected by the curb outside the Commonwealth Bank. There were perhaps fifteen of us ranged around a woman who sat on a folding chair and hugged a piano accordion. We all had a certain *look*, which was as identifiable in its own way as the look of Patrick Murphy's sheila. My dress was . . . well, *ladylike*, I wore flat heels, I might as well have been branded. I hoped only that my face (unspoiled, as our pastor would have said, by the devil's paintbox) might blend indistinguishably with the colourless air.

At the moment of Patrick Murphy's appearance, my father had the megaphone in his hand and was offering the peace that passeth understanding to all the lost who rushed hither and thither before us, not knowing where they were going.

The theatregoers, their sense of direction thus set at nought, appeared to me incandescent with goodwill, the light of weekend in their eyes. I (for whom Friday night was the most dreaded night of a circumscribed week) watched them as a starving waif might peer through a restaurant window.

"I speak not of the pleasures of this world, which are fleeting," my father said through the megaphone. "Not as the world giveth, give I unto you . . . "

Patrick Murphy and his sheila had drawn level with the Commonwealth Bank. Dear God, I prayed, let the gutter swallow me up. Let the heavens open. Let not Patrick Murphy see me.

Patrick Murphy stopped dead in his tracks and a slow grin of recognition lit his face. I squirmed with mortal shame, I could feel the heat rash on my cheeks.

"Jesus," laughed his sheila, snapping her gum. "Will ya look at those Holy Rollers."

"They got guts," said Patrick Murphy. "I always did go for guts," and he gave me the thumbs-up sign with a wink and a grin.

At Wallace Bishop's Diamond Arcade, he turned back to blow me a kiss.

It was the last time I saw him before he hitched his

motorcycle to the tailgate of a truck and got tossed under its sixteen double tyres. This happened on the Sandgate Road, near Nudgee College, and the piece in the *Courier-Mail* ran a comment by one of the priests. A bit foolhardy, perhaps, Father O'Shaughnessy said, a bit of a daredevil. Yet a brave lad, just the same, and a good one at heart. Father O'Shaughnessy could vouch for this, although he had not had the privilege, etcetera. But the lad was wearing a scapular around his neck.

Rest in peace, Patrick Murphy, I murmur, making a cross in the dust with a mango twig.

"What are you doing?" my mothers asks, smelling liturgical error.

"Doodling. Just doodling." But certain statues in churches — the Saint Peters, the faulty impetuous saints — have always had Patrick Murphy's eyes.

A few minutes later, my mother is back. "We've had a call from Miss Martin's niece in Melbourne. You remember Miss Martin? Her niece is worried. Miss Martin isn't answering her phone so we're going over." They call out from the car: "She still lives in Red Hill, we won't be long."

Miss Martin was old when I was a child. She's ninety-eight now, part of the adopted family, a network of the elderly, the lonely, the infirm, the derelict. My parents collect them. It has always been like this, and I've lost count of how many there are: people they check in on, they visit, they sit with, they take meals to. My mother writes letters for ladies with crippled arthritic hands and mails them to distant relatives who never visit. She has a long inventory of birthdays to be celebrated, she takes little gifts and cakes with candles.

By mid-afternoon she calls. "We're at the hospital. We got to her just in time. Do you mind getting your own dinner? I think we should stay with her, she'll be frightened when she regains consciousness."

They keep vigil throughout the night.

At dawn the phone wakes me. "She's gone," my mother says. "The Lord called her to be with Himself. Such a peaceful going home."

The day after the funeral, my father and I drive out to the university.

"It's not easy," he says, "trying to get a B.A. at my age."

But there is pride, just the same, in this mad scheme I have talked him into. I have always thought of him as an intellectual *manqué* whose life was interfered with by the Depression and the Gospel. (His aunts in Adelaide never recovered from the distress. "Oh your father," they said to me sadly, shaking their heads. "He was led astray." By my mother's family, they meant. "We do wish he hadn't been taken in by such a. . . . We do wish he would come back to a *respectable* religion.") And now his retirement is interfered with by all the lives that must be succoured and sustained. "It's hard to find time to study," he confesses ruefully.

People will keep on dying, or otherwise needing him.

In the university library, he leafs through books like an acolyte who has at last — after a lifetime of longing — been permitted to touch the holy objects. He strokes them with work-knotted fingers. But we are simply passing through the library today, we are on our way to meet friends of mine for lunch at the faculty club. I am privately apprehensive about this, though my father is delighted, curious, secretly flattered. He has never been in a faculty club lounge.

At the table reserved for us the waiter is asking, "Red or white, sir?" and my heart sinks. The air is full of greeting and reminiscence, but I am waiting for my father's inevitable gesture, the equivalent of the megaphone outside the Commonwealth Bank. I am bracing myself to stay calm, knowing I will be as angered by the small patronising smiles of my old friends as by my father's compulsion to "bear witness". He will turn his wineglass upside down at the very least; possibly he will make some mild moral comment on alcohol; he may offer the peace that passeth understanding to the faculty club at large.

He does none of these things.

To my astonishment, he permits the waiter to fill his glass with white wine. He is bemused, I decide, by his surroundings. And yet twice during the course of the meal, he takes polite sips from his glass.

The magnitude of this gesture overwhelms me. I have to excuse myself from the table for ten minutes.

For a week I have cunningly avoided being home with my parents for dinner, but the moment of reckoning has come. We are all here, brothers and sisters-in-law and nieces and nephews, an exuberantly affectionate bunch.

The table has been cleared now, and my father has reached for the Bible. A pause. I feel like a gladiator waiting for the lions, all the expectant faces turned towards me. It is time. The visitor always chooses the Bible reading, the visitor reads; and then my father leads family prayer.

It should be a small thing. In anyone else's home I would endure it with docile politeness.

It cannot be a concession anywhere near as great as my father's two sips of wine — a costly self-damning act.

It should be a small thing for me to open the Bible and read. There is no moral principle at stake.

Yet I cannot do it.

"I am sorry," I say quietly, hating myself.

Outside I hug the mango tree and weep for the kind of holy innocence that can inflict appalling damage; and because it is clear that they, the theologically rigid, are more forgiving than I am.

But I also move out of the shaft of light that falls from the house, knowing, with a rush of annoyance, that if they see me weeping they will discern the Holy Spirit who hovers always with his bright demanding wings.

I lean against the dark side of the mango tree and wait. A flying fox screeches in the banana clump. Gloating, the Holy Spirit whispers: *Behold the foxes, the little foxes, that spoil the vines*. One by one, the savaged bananas fall, thumping softly on the grass. From the window the sweet evening voices drift out in a hymn. The flying fox, above me, arches his black gargoyle wings.

Morgan Morgan

My grandfather, Morgan Morgan, was a yodeller and a breeder of dahlias. On Collins Street and Bourke Street, I could tug at his hand and implore "Please, Grandpa, please!" and he would throw back his head and do something mysterious in his throat and his yodel would unfurl itself like a silk ribbon. All the trams in Melbourne would come to a standstill, entangled. Bewitched pedestrians stopped and stared. But this was nothing compared with former powers: when he was a young man on the goldfields, handsome and down on his luck, the girls for miles around would come running. Yodel-o-o-o, my grandfather would sing, snaring them, winding them in. The girls would sigh and sway like cobras in the strands of his voice. He was a charmer.

"Get along with you, Morg. You're bad for business," Mrs Blackburn would say. Flowers bloomed by the bucketful around her. She would lean across roses and carnations, she would catch at his sleeve. "Here's a daisy for the nipper," and she'd tuck it behind my ear. She didn't want him to move on at all, even I knew that. "Your grandpa," she had said to me often enough, "is a fine figure of a man, they don't make men like him anymore." She'd pull one of her carnations from a bucket and swing the stem in her fingers. "A gentleman is a gentleman," she'd sigh.

"Even if he is poor as a church mouse and never found a thimbleful of gold."

It was not entirely true, Grandpa told me, that he'd never struck it rich on the goldfields — the *Kalgoorlie* goldfields, he'd say, with a loving hesitation on the *o*'s and *l*'s, a rallentando which intimated that music had gone from the language since The Rush petered out.

In those exotic and demented times, men were obsessed with the calibration of luck. Not Morgan Morgan. While other men mapped out their fevers with calipers, measuring the likely run of a seam from existing strikes, Grandpa Morgan simply watched for the aura. Wherever the aura settled, he panned or dug.

"Crazy as a bandicoot," the publican told him. "You've got to have a *system*, mate!"

But Morgan Morgan knew that gold was a gift, it never came to men of system, never had. "King David danced before the Lord," he pointed out, "which goes to show; and his gold mines were the richest in the world, I read it somewhere, some archaeologist bloke has proved it." Grandpa had his own methods of fossicking, in scripture or creek bed, it was all the same to him. He found what he wanted, or at any rate learned to want what he found.

He laboured at strings of waterholes that were known to be panned out. He was after the Morgan Nugget. This was how it appeared to him in a vision: as big as a man's fist, blackened, gnarled like a prune, cobwebby with the roots of creek ferns. He expected its presence to be announced by an echo of Welsh choirs in the tea-tree and eucalypt scrub. And it was, it was. One day, with the strains of *Cwm Rhondda* all around him, he scratched at a piece of rock with a broken fingernail and the sun caught the gash and almost blinded him.

"Solid gold," he told me. "And big as a man's fist." Not for the first time, he knew himself to be a man of destiny.

"What did you do with it, Grandpa?" I was full of awe. When he spoke of the past, I heard the surf of the delectable world of turbulence that raged beyond our garden wall. We were still at the old place in Ringwood then, across from the railway station. If I buried my face in the box-hedge of golden privet, I could hear the rush of Grandpa's life, the trains careering past to Mitcham and Box Hill and Richmond. He would listen too, leaning into the sound, and I would see his eyes travel on beyond Richmond, beyond Footscray even, out towards the unfenceable Nullarbor Plain and Kalgoorlie.

"What did you do with it, Grandpa?"

"With what?" he would ask from far away.

"With the Morgan Nugget?"

"I put it down again," he said, "right back down where I found it, inside the vision. It's still waiting just where I put it. Listen," he said, "if you put your ear to the Morgan Dahlia, you can hear it waiting."

I buried my ear in those soft salmon ruchings of petals and heard the deep hush of the past. And then *pop*, *pop*: he pinched the calix with his fingers. "That's the sound of the Morgan Nugget," he said, "when it gets impatient. It's waiting for one of us to find it again."

"Dad!" Grandma Morgan, with a basket of eggs on her arm, came down the path from the hen house. "Don't confuse the child with your nonsense." She lifted her eyebrows at me. "Always could talk the leg off an iron pot, your Grandpa."

"Pot calling the kettle black, I'd say," he grumbled. He hated to be listened in on; I hated it too. I didn't like the way the Morgan history drooped at the edges when other people were around.

Grandma Morgan was picking mint and tossing the sprigs into her basket. The leaves lay green and vivid against the eggs. "Came to tell you the pension cheques have arrived," she said.

"Well, praise be," said Grandpa, mollified. "Praise be. There's corn in Egypt yet. And on top of that," he whispered, as she moved off towards the house, "the Morgan Nugget's still waiting."

"Dad! No more nonsense. That child is never going to know the difference between truth and lies, you mark my words."

"Got eyes in the back of her head," Grandpa grumbled. "And ears in the wind. No flies on her, no siree."

It was one of his favourite sayings: *No flies on so-and-so, no siree*. To me it implied an opposite state, an unsavory kind of person, stupid, sticky, smelling overly sweet in the manner of plums left on the ground beneath our tree for too long. I imagined this person — the person on whom there *were* flies — to be pale and bloated, and to have bad breath and unwashed socks.

There was a man who delivered bonemeal for the dahlia garden on whom I thought there might be flies — if only one could see him at an unguarded moment. His clothes gave off a rich rancid smell. When he laughed it was like looking into the squishy dark mush of fruit I had to collect from the lawn before a mowing. Those few teeth which the bonemeal man still had — they announced themselves like unvanquished sentinels on a crumbling rampart — were given over to a delicate vegetation. I recognised it: it was the same silky green fur that coated the fallen plums over which floated little black parasols of flies.

Yet one day, when I came out to the dahlia garden just as the bonemeal man was leaving, Grandpa Morgan was tossing his fine head of hair in the wind and laughing his fine Welsh laugh. The bonemeal man was laughing too,

trundling his barrow down our path, doubled up with
mirth between its shafts, his green teeth waving about like
banners.

"Grandpa, what is it, what is it? Why are you laughing,
Grandpa?"

"Oh," Grandpa gasped, patting me on the head in the
way that meant a subject was not for discussing. "No flies
on *him*, no siree."

This was the best thing: I could always count on Grandpa
Morgan to be outrageous. That was the word people used:
the neighbours, my grandmother, my mother, my uncles.
"He's *outrageous*," they would say, shaking their heads
and throwing up their hands and smiling.

If I asked him to, he would yodel in the schoolyard
when he came to fetch me, and abracadabra, we two were
the hub of a circle of awed envy. When I passed the Teachers' Room at morning tea time, I'd hear the older ones
whisper and smile: "That's Morgie's granddaughter."

On our walks he would stop and talk to everyone we
met, "to *anyone*, anyone at all," Uncle Cyril would groan.
He spoke to the butcher, the baker, the lady in the cake
shop, to men who did shady undiscussable things, even
men who smelled of horses and *took bets*, whatever that
was.

"What can you be thinking of?" Grandma would say,
"with the child hearing every word? A man *known* to be
mixed up with off-course betting."

I knew bets to be deeply evil. I imagined them to be
huge and ravenous and almost hidden behind fearful
masks. Once upon a time, in Kalgoorlie, Grandpa himself
had made bets, but that was before the Lord saved him
and showed him the light. Now, he said, he only bet on the
Day of Judgement. Still, he couldn't see any harm in
talking to people who "knew horses." He would introduce

me. "This is Paddy," he would say; "a man who knows horses if ever anyone did." I myself had no interest in knowing horses on account of their large and alarming teeth, but I rather liked those brave horse-knowing men.

Sometimes Grandma, shocked, would call out: "Dad! I want to have a word with you, Dad." From the front window, she would have watched us coming over the bridge from the Ringwood Station. The most *interesting* people came off the trains and walked over that bridge. Grandma would have seen us stop and talk to some gentleman who wore string, perhaps, for suspenders, and whose shoes were stuffed in an intricate way with newspapers, and who gave off the rank smell of the pubs. "Dad!" she would say. "What are you *thinking* of, to introduce the child to such strangers?"

"Strangers?" Grandpa would raise his eyebrows in surprise. "That wasn't a stranger. That was Bluey McTavish from back of Geelong. We don't know any strangers."

This was certainly true, though we'd only just met Mr Bluey McTavish of Geelong, whose life history we would discuss over the sorting of dahlia bulbs. I don't know what it was about Grandpa Morgan, but people told him a great deal about themselves very quickly. "There aren't any such people as strangers," he told me. "Or if there are, I've never met them."

"I don't know what's going to come of that child," Grandma Morgan said, throwing up her hands and trying not to smile. "But one thing's certain: she'll never know the difference between truth and lies."

Grandpa said with ruffled dignity: "One thing she'll know about is dahlias."

The dahlias, the dahlias. They stretched to the edge of the world. When I stood between the rows, I saw nothing but jungle, with great suns of flowers above me, so heavy they nodded on their stalks and shone down through the forests of their own leaves. Such a rainbow of suns: from creamy white to a purple that was almost black. The dahlias believed in excess: they could never have too many petals. The dahlia which could crowd the most pleatings of pure light about its centre won a blue ribbon at the Melbourne Show. It was an article of faith with us that some year the Morgan Dahlia would win that ribbon.

Grandpa Morgan did things to the bulbs and the soil. He married broad-petalled pinks to pin-tucked yellows; he introduced sassy purples to smocked whites with puffed sleeves and lacy hems. He watched over his nurslings, he crooned to them, he prayed. To birds and snails, he issued strong Welsh warnings (the Lord having taken away a certain range of Australian vocabulary). As his flowerlings grew, he murmured endearments; and they gathered themselves up into a delirium of pleats, rank upon rank of petals, tier upon tier, frilled prima donnas. The colour of the Morgan dahlia was a salmon that could make judges weep, the salmon of a baby's cheek, the colour of a lover's whisper. And it did win yellow ribbons, and red, at the Melbourne Show, but never the coveted blue.

"Is it waiting till we find the Morgan Nugget again?" I asked.

"Very likely," Grandpa said. "Very likely."

The day Grandma came out with the news of Uncle Charlie, we were deep in dahlias.

"Dad," she said. "Charlie's gone."

Grandpa paused in mid-weeding. A clump of clover and crabgrass dangled from between his fingers. He sank down on the ground between the dahlias and rested his head in his hands. "Well," he said, sadly and slowly. "Charlie. So Charlie went first."

"Where's he gone?" I wanted to know.

"Uncle Charlie's gone to heaven," Grandma told me, and Grandpa said: "He's dead." He pushed his trowel into the soil and lifted up a handful of earth. It was alive with ants and worms, we watched it move in the palm of his hand. "I'm next," he sighed, and he smelled the earth and held it for me to smell, and he rubbed it against his cheek as though it were a kitten. "I'm next, I suppose."

"Next for what?"

"Next for dying," he said.

"What happens when you die, Grandpa?"

"They put you in a box and they bury you under the ground with the dahlia bulbs."

I stared at him in horror. "Uncle Charlie should run away and hide."

"You can't run away when you're dead," he said.

"Grandpa," I whispered, beginning to shiver, "will they do it to you?"

"Yes," he said.

"And to me?"

I crept between his earth-covered arms and he held me tightly and rocked me back and forth between the dahlias. "Yes," he sighed, "one day, yes. That's the way it is. But then we'll be with the Lord."

I didn't want to be with the Lord. I had a brilliant idea. "Grandpa," I said, "we'll run away *before* we die. I know a very good place in the woodshed, they'd never find us."

"Dad!" Grandma's voice steamed over with exasperation. "Now just what have you been telling her this time? How will that child ever know the difference between truth and a lie? Uncle Charlie," she said to me, "has gone straight to heaven, and that is the simple truth."

Mr Peabody knew the truth. Every Sunday it spoke in his bones, it shook him from head to foot.

There must have been some obscure and ancient rule at

church. It must have been this rule which forced Mr
Peabody, week after week, to sit directly in front of
Grandpa Morgan. Mr Peabody was a tiny man, elderly,
and seemingly frail as a sparrow, though he must have had
enormous reserves of stamina on which to draw.

Behind him, sheltering in the leeside of the Spirit of the
Lord as it blustered and rushed through Grandpa, my
little brother and I kept score. When the spirit moved,
Grandpa shouted *hallelujah* in his fine Welsh voice. The
shock waves hit Mr Peabody sharply in the nape of his
neck and travelled down his spine with such force that he
would rise an inch or two from the pew. Most of his body
would go rigid, but his head and his hands would quiver
for seconds at a time. *Glory, glory*, he would murmur in a
terror-stricken prayerful voice.

These seismic interludes infused Sundays with extraordinary interest. And there was also this: from monitoring
the passions of Mr Peabody, my brother and I learned
self-control, the ability to tamp down an explosion of
mirth and turn it into a mere telegraphed signal of gleaming eyes and a coded numerology of fingers.

But then came the day that a shaft of sunlight fell from
a high amber-glass window in the church and placed a
crown of gold on Mr Peabody's head. "Oh!" I gasped
aloud. "*Look!*" And Grandpa shouted *Hallelujah!* and
Mr Peabody rose up into his corona like a skyrocket and I
saw a million golden doves and the gilded petals of all the
dahlias in the world rising up into the pointed arch above,
where God lived.

"It was the Holy Spirit you saw," the pastor told me.
"The Holy Spirit descending as a dove."

"Going *up*," I corrected. "Lots and lots of them, and
dahlias too."

"The Holy Spirit," he said again, less certainly. "In the
form of a dove."

"I'm not so sure," my Sunday School teacher said. "She makes things up."

"Out of the mouths of babes," the pastor reminded her.

"She makes things up," my Sunday School teacher insisted. "She handles the truth very carelessly. She believes her own lies."

"Grandpa," I asked, "how can you tell the difference between truth and a lie?"

He was working bonemeal into the soil around his dahlias; over us nodded those heavy salmon suns. He went on kneading the rich black loam, intent on his labour.

Apprehensively I persisted: "Is the Morgan Nugget true?"

He went on sifting the soil.

I thought hopefully: perhaps he made up death.

"The truth," he said at last, "shall make you free. John, chapter 8, verse 32."

"Grandpa," I said, "there were doves with gold wings, and dahlias too. Mr Peabody made them fly. I saw them."

"I know you did."

I leaned towards him. "And the Morgan Nugget?" I breathed.

"Is true," he said. "Is true."

The Bloody Past, The Wandering Future

"The bloody past!" my great-grandfather swore. "The interfering bloody past!" He was half stunned with incredulity and whisky, not so far gone as to damage the crisp Oxford edges of his vowels, but enough to make him grateful for the embankment railings. He leaned against them and pushed the matted bougainvillaea furiously aside as though slamming a door. He made a fist and brandished it. *Litera scripta manet*, his fist said. (After two drinks he sweated Latin, and he'd had whisky for breakfast as usual.) "It was the Grammar School money, wasn't it? That's how you traced me. From those bloody remittance cheques! Isn't that so?"

"Yes," the young man (my Grandfather Turner) said simply. Most of his eighteen years he had been rehearsing this moment. He stood waiting for his life to change irrevocably. Certain details he never forgot: the muddled alcoholic stink of his father's black gown, the runnels of sweat leaking out from under the preposterous wig (now slightly askew), the cascade of damp legal curls dripping onto the starched collar. Ever after, he could not so much as catch sight of a barrister or a Queen's Counsel without feeling this same lurching of the earth beneath his feet.

As for my great-grandfather, the drunken barrister, I

suppose that visions of the Eastbourne Pier and his wife's face, and the English Channel back of both, must have flooded his memory with the suddenness of aneurysms bursting. He actually moaned and put a hand to his forehead, though all he could see, between the railings and the bougainvillaea, was the Brisbane River winding its slow unhistorical way to the sea.

In a matter of weeks that same river, in that same torpid fin-de-siècle January, would astound my great-grandfather and several thousand other people, hurling itself down like a dingo on the little fold of Brisbane, laying waste much of the city and drowning my great-grandfather and the interfering past as deeply as he ever could have wished.

But on the day of which I speak, a few weeks before the flood, there was a moment when he hesitated before that past as before a door opened in a dark alley. He stared at the son who had come halfway around the world to find him. Seconds, maybe whole minutes, ticked by in the swooning air.

"What is it you want?" he asked at last.

My grandfather was not able to answer this question with words, though years later he wished he had asked why. Simply: *Why?* Then again, he was often relieved he had not.

Beads of perspiration gleamed on the barrister's eyebrows and hung in dewdrops from the tips of his juridical curls. He straightened his spine against the embankment railings and stared, puzzled, into the crimson throats of the bougainvillaea. He made a large, vague, sweeping gesture of disbelief. "This too may pass," he said. His gesture took in the splendid colonial Court House, the unpaved street, the slatternly river, the heat. Even in the face of absurdity, his gesture implied, a gentleman — especially a decaying gentleman — must never lose his composure.

"I should think we are in agreement," he said courteously, "that this was a mistake."

Then he nodded politely and walked away, the black gown lifting and dipping like damp wings.

My grandfather had to lean against the railings and the bougainvillaea. He stood and watched until there was no further point in doing so. A few weeks later the spot where he had been standing — so he judged from the newspaper photographs — was covered with fifteen feet of warm mud and raging water. My grandfather fancied, in retrospect, that he had known, had had a precognitive glimpse of chaos. But he had blinked it away and turned round and gone back to Melbourne. He was in a hurry. He was, in fact, in such urgent need of a new purpose for his life that almost immediately he set about becoming the kind of patriarch he had fantasised he would find: scholarly, devoted to the family, touched by tragedy. He did not wait for the boat back to England. He married and put out roots right there where he was, begetting sons and daughters.

And in Brisbane, if my great-grandfather had second thoughts, the river left no record of it.

My visitants. At certain seasons they catch me unawares: when return passages are booked, when passports must be renewed. I wake, sometimes, in the middle of the night, heart pounding, and listen to the seconds changing places, a dizzy quadrille.

This summer, my son turns eighteen. (My great-grandfather laughs his whisky laugh. *You too*, he says, with a polite but sardonic smile, *you too will pass*. His consonants cut like crystal, his vowels are solid sterling, pure cashmere. *You are losing your Australian accent*, he comments, pursing his lips. *Not that your present accent — whatever it is — is any improvement*.)

He says: *I was the age that you are now, and my son was the age of your son, when the river threw its tantrum.*

I am as far from Brisbane as it is possible — *sub luna* — to be, though I expect, in this summer of my son's eighteenth birthday, to lean against the bougainvillaea again and stare at the river. When I myself was eighteen I stood there often enough, a moony undergraduate, waiting for the university bus, reading the river, listening for the future that would sweep me off my feet.

Who will unravel the routes and reasons of my nomadic life? — though they are no more convoluted, I suppose, than the reasons which led my great-grandfather to abandon, overnight, a wife and young son and a respectable law practice in Eastbourne, that most proper of English cities.

From the window above my desk I gaze out, bemused, at the river — the St. Lawrence River. Down at the bottom of my yard, it sucks away at the base of our cliffs: plucks and thaws, plucks and thaws. I live at the desiccating edge of things, on the dividing line between two countries, nowhere.

My grandfather's face, pensive, hangs in the maples like a moon. *Never*, he begs, *never live on the banks of a river*.

This is very high ground, I assure him. *Sixty feet of limestone between me and the water*.

My great-grandfather comes lurching through the trees, avoiding his son. He laughs his well-bred English laugh. He laughs his turn-of-the-century Brisbane tavern laugh. *This too will pass*, he promises.

After the Second World War, when my father came home from the Air Force, jobs were not so easy to come by in Melbourne. Too many returning soldiers and new immigrants from Europe, I suppose. When an offer of work came from Brisbane there was no question about whether we would go, though neighbours and relations, stunned, all said: "Brisbane! You can't be serious?"

"When you buy a house," warned my grandfather, "buy on high ground, and well away from the river."

But memory is short. In Brisbane my grandfather's advice was thought to be quaint and neurotic. Just the same, my father would not look at a house near the river, nor one that was not on high ground. He had cause to be grateful in Christmas '74 when the river got up to its old tricks, thrashing around like a dragon in fitful sleep.

"There's a purpose behind everything," my father told me by trans-Pacific phone call on the morning following the disaster. My father is a deeply religious man. "Sometimes we have to wait a long time, almost a century in fact, to know what was in the mind of God."

"Dad," I say awkwardly. My father and I have, for a long time now, avoided discussing many topics, especially such matters as what may be on the mind of God. "Everyone's safe, then?"

"Hardly everyone," he says with a hint of reproach. "But your parents and your brothers and their families are safe. We're all pitching in with the relief work, everyone is, it's fantastic. I thought you'd want to know we're okay, in case you saw something on the news." Then he laughs, self-deprecatingly: "Though I don't suppose Brisbane . . . over there. I suppose we don't count for too much in the big wide world." There is a silence and then he laughs again. "If you could see me! Mud from head to toe. But it isn't funny. It's awful, it's tragic seeing them crammed into schools and churches. They look so dazed."

"Dad . . ." I say, but am awash in old places, my old schools, the university bus stop, the park on the river bank where I had my first kiss.

"The water's receding now," my father says. "The

worst's over. But it'll be *days* . . . and the *mud!* Heaven knows how long before the mud will be cleared away. I wonder if Brisbane will ever look the same again. I wonder if anyone will stay."

People do stay, of course.

They even — amazing as it seems — build right on the river bank again.

As for us, for my expatriate husband and myself, the mere thought of Brisbane almost ceasing to be did something to us. We couldn't afford it, but we had to go home — come home — that summer; the *northern* summer, that is — though it was a mild and sweet-smelling winter in Brisbane, and the wattles were in bloom along the river.

"Since 'ow long 'ave you been in Canada?" asks the telephone voice from the Australian High Commission in Ottawa. It is a French Canadian voice, heavily accented, but I long ago gave up expecting the logical in matters such as this.

"Much longer than I expected," I answer.

"Why did you come?"

"Academic reasons." In both senses, I think. "It wasn't planned, really. It just arrived."

"*Il est arrivé?*" she says, thrown slightly off course.

"*C'est ça. Exactement,*" I assure her. "Look, is this relevant to the renewal of my Australian passport?"

"Yes," she says. "Why do you stay 'ere?"

"Stahier?"

"*Au Canada.*"

"Ah. For the same academic reasons. I really can't see what this has to . . ."

"Before we can renew your Australian passport," she explains . . . (and I puzzle over that plural. Who is this French Canadian Australian *we*?) . . . "Before we can renew, you 'ave to sign a document authorising us to conduct a search of Canadian immigration files. As long as you 'ave never applied for Canadian citizenship, there is *pas de problème.*"

"How nice," I say, cut to the quick. And hear my great-grandfather's laugh.

Television had just come to Brisbane in 1953, though no families we knew could afford a set. For the coronation, we loaded folding chairs into family cars and drove into the city and sat outside shop windows to watch as Her Majesty arrived at Westminster Abbey. It was all very festive.

I remember the backyard parties, the fireworks, the decorations. Ours were splendid, especially on the garage, a corrugated-iron structure that slumped against the banana clump. A mango tree leaned over its rotting wooden doors, which we had festooned — my brothers and I — with red, white, and blue; with the Royal Ensign, the Union Jack, the Southern Cross. ELIZABETH REGINA, in huge wobbly letters, picked its way across the undulating wall. Below this, stretching all the way from the mango tree to the banana palms, was a long accordion-pleated poster (we had all been given them in school) of the Royal Coach and the horses and the footmen and the Crown Jewels and each item of the coronation regalia, especially that part of the royal hemline where the Golden Wattle was embroidered.

"Magnificent!" my father said.

He was, I recall, deeply moved, perhaps by the ingenuity and acrobatic skill that had been involved in climbing the mango tree and springing across to the garage roof in order to hang the bunting. He put his hand on my shoulder. He never held it against me (not even, I truly believe, in secret) that I, his firstborn, was a daughter. "Tradition," he said, and I was both curious and embarrassed

about the huskiness in his voice. "We have to know where
we come from. My own father and grandfather . . . "

He went astray in his thoughts and I had to prompt him.

"Did Grandpa ever see the old King?"

"He saw the old *Queen* once, Victoria. He was very
young, it was before his father . . . . Your great-
grandfather, I'm afraid, was a scoundrel, but still, even
he . . . . There was money that kept coming for your
grandfather to go to Grammar School. All those years
when nobody knew where . . . so even he had a sense
of . . . "

There was a long silence.

"Well, anyway, now we belong here," he said. "*Here*."
He looked at our little wooden house, and the rusty iron
garage, and the gravel tracks of the driveway, and the old
Bedford van, and the mango tree and the passionfruit
vines hanging matted over the fences. He took a deep
princely breath of that damp and heavy air, and I remember thinking with a thrill of proprietary power: How *rich*
we are!

"This is the place where we belong," he said. "You'll
always belong here. And your children. And your children's children."

About me, I think, he was right. But perhaps it was
only to be expected that I would be nomadic. Perhaps it
was in my blood.

My son and I are walking beside the Charles River in
Cambridge, Massachusetts, because — for the time being
— I am teaching at M.I.T.

"Well," he says, "I've decided on the University of
Toronto."

"I'm glad," I tell him. "I'm glad we'll still all be living
in the same country. Well," I correct myself sheepishly,
gesturing at Boston, "most of the time, that is."

My son shrugs and grins at me. He finds me unnecessarily anxious about separations. Movement is the norm of his life.

My son seems to me very American. Or very Canadian perhaps. That is to say, unlike me, he has an easy confidence that the world is manageable. He is not unduly bothered by absurdity. The random and irrational do not cause him anxiety. This, it seems to me, is because of his birth and his many subsequent summers in Los Angeles. He seems to me very Californian. Or perhaps very Canadian.

I have a vivid memory of walking with my Grandfather Turner in the Ballarat Gardens, not far from Melbourne. It was before we moved to Brisbane, so I must have been five or six. We must have gone walking in the Gardens quite often because there are several photographs of us — black and white, not too clear — here and there in family collections.

My grandfather does not look in the least like other Australian grandfathers. He wears a tweed suit with a vest and watch chain. He carries an elegant walking stick. He is holding my hand. I am wearing the long golden corkscrew curls which I hate but which everyone else considers adorable. I am also wearing one of the little dresses with smocked bodices which I frequently rip while climbing trees.

The paths of the Ballarat Gardens are lined with statues. My grandfather, who was the school headmaster until he retired, plays a game with me.

"This one?" he asks, pointing with his stick.

"That's Mercury."

"And this one?"

"That's the Venus de Milo."

"And this one?"

"That's Persephone."

"And why is Persephone weeping?"

"She misses ... I forget her name. She misses her mother."

"Demeter," he says. "She misses her mother Demeter. And she wants to go back. Whichever world she's in, she always misses the other one and wants to go back."

We emerge from the avenue of statues at the shore of the Ballarat Lake. We walk out on the little wooden jetty.

"When I was little," my grandfather says, "about as old as you are now, my father used to take me walking on the Eastbourne Pier. Just like this."

I already know (because with grandfather all conversations are lessons of one kind or another) that Eastbourne is in England and that England is on the other side of the world, a place as easily imagined and as fabulous as Persephone's Underworld. We sit on the end of the jetty and I swing my legs back and forth and throw pebbles in the water.

"Look at the dragonflies," my grandfather says, pointing. But there is something in his voice.

"Grandpa?" I ask curiously. "What's the matter?"

He doesn't answer, but he puts his walking stick carefully down on the jetty, and takes me on his lap and holds me so tightly it hurts.

Isobars

A Fugue on Memory

Where does a circle start? Wherever one decides. All these circles begin and end in Melbourne.

And what is an isobar? An isobar is an imaginary line connecting places of equal pressure on a map. All lines on a map, we must acknowledge, are imaginary; they are ideas of order imposed on the sloshing flood of time and space. Lines on a map are talismanic and represent the magical thinking of quantitative and rational people.

These particular isobars connect points where the pressure of memory exerts an equivalent force.

And how is a storm front plotted? The detection of warm fronts, cold fronts, rainstorms, cyclones, and other such assorted cataclysms and disasters requires the intuition of the scientist. If the meteorologist has received sufficient advance training in oceanography, statistical mathematics, Jungian archetypes and dreams, he or she will be able to read the signs correctly. Such a meteorologist will watch for the figure in the surface disturbance of water (though to what purpose, discerning the gust in a shoal of lake breezes, no one is ever certain).

Water

The Ringwood Lake and the Ballarat Lake were separate bodies of water in the Jurassic Period, early 1940s, when M (for Made in Melbourne, maid in Melbourne, for memory itself, for meteorologist-in-training, for . . .). But perhaps we should be more conventional and call her Em? Or even, more decorously, more appropriately, buttoning our gloves and keeping our knees together in the approved Melbourne manner, Emily. Yes, Emily will do very nicely . . .

The Ringwood Lake and the Ballarat Lake were separate bodies of water when Emily floated the leaves of childhood on them, when she threw breadcrusts to swans now several generations gone. But those two ponds, infinite as oceans in a bygone era, are one puddle now. Statues clutter the walks that surround them. Sometimes the English grandfather comments on the statues, sometimes the Welsh grandfather. The Ringwood town hall and the Ballarat cathedral and the Ringwood railway station push through bullrushes.

The English grandfather's hand is soft and pale, a schoolmaster's hand; the Welshman's is callused. With a grandfather at each side like charms at her wrists, Emily flexes her toes, she sinks her bare feet into gurgling mud. Already she is learning that the property of water is sameness, Ringwood shimmering, Ballarat dreaming, the future sighing at its own reflection.

Once, the English grandfather says, there was a picnic by the lake and afterwards you vomited chocolate in the back seat of the Bishop of Ballarat's car. Your mother was mortified.

The Welsh grandfather says: Don't lean so far out from the edge of the jetty, the swans will snap at your fingers. Once there was a picnic — don't you remember? — where a little boy fell in and drowned. His mother sobbed and sobbed, she could not be comforted, she had to be taken away.

The English grandfather scoops up lakewater and pours it into Emily's palm. One little drop of memory, he says, can hold everything at once, and forever. It's like having a thousand eyes.

Grandpa, she says. Why is that lady crying? And what is that man doing?

What lady? both the grandfathers say. What man? Where?

There, she says. There. Over there by the gum tree. Is she the little boy's mother?

Oh, they say, maybe. Or maybe she's someone else. In any case, it's nothing, it's nothing that little girls need to worry their pretty heads about.

But Grandpa, Emily persists, why is she crying?

No, no, she's not crying, they say. (Their voices are fearful, embarrassed, harsh.) She's laughing. Trust us, they say. Don't look.

And they take her hands, playful, and lift and swing, this is fun, they swing her to kingdom come, out out over the water, over the Pacific, over the Atlantic, over the Arabian Sea

where, briefly, the fisherman offers his hand as she steps into his boat. She is in South India, Pleistocene era, 1970s, the coconut palms throwing spidery shadows on Kovalam beach. When she takes the fisherman's hand, brown flesh white flesh interlaced, he giggles with embarrassment, waits for her to settle herself between the lashed logs, pushes off with his bamboo paddle.

Blood warm water bathes her from the waist down. The boat is stable and buoyant, not watertight; she and the fisherman ride just below the water's surface, passing through the sides of waves as a knife through butter, as spirits through walls, as memory through time. She sees Ringwood swans and a row of little fishes suspended like bubbles in a green flank of the Arabian Sea. The Bishop of Ballarat, concerned, leans forward with his bamboo paddle. You won't be sick, will you? he asks in some unknown tongue. The ways of God are inscrutable, he says; it is not our place to question why. Don't lean so far, he says. Someone was drowned doing that.

Why is that woman screaming? she calls, her mouth full of water. And what is the man doing with the knife?

What knife? the fisherman shouts back. (Bubbles and tiny fish stream from his lips like ribbons.) Where? he calls.

There, she points. There. On the beach.

No, no, you are not understanding, the fisherman says. Man is cleaning fish and woman is laughing, isn't it?

Relieved, she smiles through the fluid green belly of the wave as the fisherman casts his net. His eyes and hers are both amber as cats'-eyes in the water, salt crusts their lashes, branches of their seaweed hair float into the mouths of crabs. Bubbles of laughter fizz from her throat, it's a champagne baptism, euphoric, surf foaming through her lips, and the woman on the beach is laughing too, thank God (yet it is odd the way a laugh or a scream seems defined by the ears of the hearer). Still. The fisherman knows the local language, he must be right

though people do tell lies, Thoreau warns. Especially the avoiders, especially those fearful of being held accountable for what they have failed to do, especially those ashamed of their own fear.

Thoreau is sitting at the edge of the water, his hut behind him, nine beanrows and a hive for the honeybee to one side, Walden Pond flashing sunlight in his eyes.

The man over there under the trees, she says. The one talking to the woman who is crying . . .

Thoreau looks and looks away. They say she has lost a child, he says. They say she has never been quite right since. And the man is offering comfort, he's promising extravagant things. Thoreau shakes his head and warns: But men rarely mean what they say. Still, he adds, the woman wants to believe him. Can't you hear her laughter?

It's such a strange laugh, Emily says. It doesn't sound like a laugh at all, it sounds more like a —

Thoreau puts a finger to his lips. If you hear a different drum, he says, you have a choice. You can march to it, though this will certainly get you into difficulties with the authorities. Or you can pretend you didn't hear it, like everyone else. You have to weigh the consequences, you have to choose, you have to balance costs,

balance is essential. Left foot on one ice cake, right foot on another, no one should be too far from shore when playing this game. Five minutes, so they say, at these temperatures, and the body shuts down.

But warmth is on the way, April is here, the Ice Age is over, spring has come to the frozen St Lawrence, a rubble of ice with a Great Lakes postmark is floating past Emily's dock and should reach Montreal by the middle of May. A puzzled loon, the first of the season, touches down, disappears, surfaces, watches the mad balancing act.

Don't lean so far when you throw him a crust, the Welsh grandfather says. A boy was drowned doing that.

Do I hear a woman scream, Emily asks herself, puzzled. Or is it simply one fractious chunk of ice shrieking up against another?

Newspapers

The Melbourne *Age*, the *Sun*, the *Argus* all have pictures: of the little boy who drowned, of the mother weeping, of the murdered woman. Was this all the same event? Emily, remembering a picnic by the lake and much panic, is confused. Her parents and grandparents press their lips together and shake their heads. Her mother says: Don't ever lean out from the dock, don't ever *ever* go in the water unless someone is with you.

A man on the Ringwood railway station tells Emily's grandfather: I expect she asked for it. (The mother? Emily wonders. Or the woman with the knifestripes on her stomach?) Newspapers flutter from carriage windows and shout from their stands beside the ticket grille. These are the facts, the newspapers say. Women and children are always asking for trouble. They get it.

Brisbane *Courier-Mail*, circa 1953. BETTY SHANKS MURDERED. This happened just an eyeblink away from Wilston State School. In the playground, rumours fly. *She had boyfriends, she talked to strange men*. From the school gates, the children can see the police, the reporters, the chalk outline on the footpath.

It seems, the teacher tells the frightened (yet strangely excited) children, that Betty Shanks rode home on the tram late at night. She was all alone. She spoke to a strange man. This was madness on the part of Betty Shanks.

Don't ever speak to strange men, the teacher warns. Don't ever go out alone at night.

If you do, the nice constable tells the class, you're asking for trouble.

The *TLS* (May 5, 1988) has reviews and scholarly reminders that the victim is always to blame. "Tuberculosis attacks failures," declares medical expert of 1912. (*TLS*, page 463, a review of a book by F.B. Smith, the Australian medical historian.) "It is just the ignorance of millions like yourself that causes the miseries of mankind," Smith reports that a grieving mother was told over the body of her dead tubercular child.

The woman weeps and weeps. She's a difficult woman, the doctors and experts say. Probably overprotective, stifling, the usual thing. Probably *caused* it, in a way; more or less programmed the child for death. A difficult woman.

CBC, Canada, the national news, May 6, 1988: A recent survey of attitudes of high school students toward rape indicates that most boys think girls who are raped were asking for it.

Air. And circles within circles

Curses fly through the air, and sometimes fists, and sometimes broken bottles. Emily stands in a circle on a street corner somewhere in the heart of Melbourne or in the vortex of Brisbane (they are one circle now: rampart, the ring of accusers, prison wall, ghetto, all the same circle). There are drunks and traffic in all directions. In the air above Emily's head, catcalls collide with Biblical codes. *Come unto me all ye who are weary* . . . leaps out of the megaphone. *Aaah, shut yer fucking mouths!* comes winging back into the circle.

Emily watches the words eddying together, twisting, full of cyclone danger.

This particular evening (Jurassic Era again, the Japanese defeated but black paint still being scraped from the windows of Melbourne), this particular evening of Circle Time, which is every evening, a ragged mother and a dirty little boy stop to watch, leaning against a shop window. The boy licks an ice-cream and watches Emily who stares back hungrily. It is his safety she wants; being part of *that* crowd, the circle outside the circle, one of the watchers. Whatever happens, the boy can stay or go. The boy is safe.

Emily wonders when the lots were drawn, when the circles were allotted, and by whom. The kind of thought that comes from beyond the margins, from who can say where? from outside the lines that form the edges of maps, the kind of question that can change worlds asks itself inside Emily's five-year-old mind: Is anyone allowed to change places? Is it against the rules? What happens if the rules or the circles are broken?

The boy licks his ice-cream and watches her. What is he thinking? She sees him suddenly suck in his breath, sees his eyes widen, sees the man with the knife. A cry with no sound to it flies from Emily's mouth.

The boy disappears behind scuffling bystanders, police, circle people. The police are angry. *Holy Rollers,* they mutter. *Asking for trouble.*

Nobody sees what happens, nobody hears.

Nobody saw, nobody heard, nothing we can do, the police tell Emily (Brisbane now, the seedy West End, 1965).

But everyone must have heard the screams, she says.

Tell us exactly . . . (The police are elaborately patient.)

Emily tries to reconstruct: a scream in the air,

screams, it is night and she is alone in the house but she rushes out to the street. (This happens much too quickly for fear or thought to intrude.) She sees the white man with the knife, the black woman screaming, the pregnant black woman screaming.

And then? the police ask.

And then, and then? Emily pounds at the blank that retroactive fear creates. The knife, the blood, the blur.

I must have run between them, she says, amazed, her hands shaking.

Emily is inside her house, bandaging the slash on the woman's arm, when the police say: Not a thing we can do, I'm afraid.

Listen, they explain to Emily (kindly, fatherly). A woman like you shouldn't get mixed up . . . *etcetera* . . . bloody lucky you didn't get yourself stabbed.

About the Abo whore, they say. (Excuse our language.) Just asking for trouble. Best to turn a deaf ear. Nobody sees, nobody hears, that's the ticket.

That's the ticket: the same old one that Kitty Genovese held when her number came up in New York, when the knife flashed, when a porridge of her screams filled the air and reached dozens of ears, but nobody saw.

Glittering, curving through air, the knife slices through a life in Boston, March 1987. The blade rests against Emily's throat, whispers to her larynx: I am steel, I am real. You may scream all you want but no one will see or hear. You've been asking for this, you deserve me.

Air! Emily gasps. Air! she pleads. Air! Fresh air!

Personally, someone (an Australian) tells Emily at a writers' conference, *I think writing about violence is in bad taste.*

You see? the knife chortles, triumphant. What did I tell you?

I'll be back, the blade whispers (a sleazy sound, cold as steel against pliant skin). In dream after dream, I'll be back.

The Last of the Hapsburgs

This is all you can see: the young woman, the Pacific, the stands of sugarcane beyond the dune grasses, and four miles of sand so firm that when Cabrisi's horse (the one that went wild, the brumby) when Cabrisi's horse gallops there, you can barely see hoofprints.

The young woman leaves no footprints at all. She stands with her feet and ankles in the erratic line of froth, at that point where ocean and shore eat each other, and reads the Port Douglas beach. Cabrisi's horse, nostrils flaring with the smell of her, rears: a salute of sorts.

"Caedmon," she says — here, the naming of creatures is all hers — "you beautiful show-off!" Of course he knows it. So bloody beautiful that a cry catches in her throat. Caedmon whinnies again, a high and jubilant note, and brushes air with his delicate forelegs. Another sign. The beach is thick with them, but who has time enough for the decoding, the translating, the recording?

Surf rises from her ankles to her knees. *Sing me North Queensland,* it lisps with its slickering tongues.

I can't, she laments, hoisting up her skirt. *I can't.*

She would need a different sort of alphabet, a

chlorophyll one, a solar one. The place will not fit into *words*.

Surf rushes between her thighs. *Sing me North Queensland*, it commands.

The young woman lifts her arms high above her head and faces the ocean. She begins to dance. She sings. When the sun slides behind Double Point, she climbs the hill at the end of the beach, still singing. She finds the track, and eventually the road, and walks until a Holden utility brakes in a skirl of dust. "Stone the crows, Miss Davenport," the driver says. "You all right?"

She looks at him, dazed. Her sodden clothes give off steam. She says vaguely: "Yes, oh yes, perfectly all right, thank you."

Driving on, the man shakes his head and mumbles to himself, not without affection: "Strange bloody old chook. A looker once, probably. Quite a looker, lay you a quid, back in her prime."

Miss Davenport, the woman thinks, blinking, as though she has just stumbled across something she had misplaced. Miss Davenport the schoolteacher. And not young at all, how odd.

Before the avocadoes and kiwi fruit and mangoes, back in the time of the sugarcane, Wednesday afternoons used to roll in with a dreadful humid regularity. They would float up from Cairns, cumulus, wet, fuzzy, drift past Yorkey's Knob and Port Douglas, and settle onto Mossman. *Wednesdays come several times a week,* Miss Davenport wrote to her sister in Brisbane. *I do think sport is very much overrated by the Department of Education. Why can't we have a compulsory afternoon of thinking instead? Or of daydreaming?*

Technically supervising the girls, Miss Davenport wilted under a parasol. *Deliquescence*, she thought. (She had a habit of fondling words.) *We are all gone into the world of fog,* she thought. Deliquescence: it had a damp sound, soft on the tongue. Miss Davenport mopped at her face with a lace-edged linen handkerchief. Flies molested her. She kept a fascinated eye on Rebecca. Already she had misplaced Hazel.

Rebecca and Hazel, she wrote to her sister, *have the gift. They are consummate artists. Houdini pales in comparison.*

Ida, her sister, lived in a flat in Toowong. Two years earlier, Ida had retired from one of Brisbane's more exclusive schools, and since then heraldry had engulfed her, the branches and twigs and epiphyte creepers of the family tree curling through her sleep, *gryphons rampant* and *fields azure* blooming in her waking thoughts. She wrote to vicars in Sussex villages and mapped her way, vine by vine and knothole by knothole, into the past. Not that this meant she neglected the scrapbooks. Far from it. At Christmas, both she and Lucia still worked on the travel book, refurbishing a June day in an Italian village here, resetting a sentence there. Emendations were also constantly made to the archival records of the more remarkable students.

You never know, Ida wrote back on the subject of the present specimens. *You just never know. Can any good thing come out of Mossman? As always, the answer is: who can possibly say? For you and me, Lucia, life is what we can catch in our scrapbook nets. That and only that, my dear. So pin your Rebecca and your Hazel right through their pretty wings with your fountain pen.*

Catch as catch can, thought Miss Davenport, dissolving beneath her parasol. There was a coded reproach in Ida's letter, but Ida had earned a permanent right to the little slinging privileges and arrows of sisterhood. Ida had hushed things up and smoothed things down the

time Lucia's life had quite shockingly spilled out of
handwritten page into messy event. Afterwards, of
course, the private girls' schools were out of the question. Afterwards, Lucia had to be grateful for appoint-
ments in such places as Childers and Mt Isa and
Mossman.

Miss Lucia Davenport could not see Hazel, but she
could still see Rebecca working her way into invisibility.
At each cheer or catcall, as though the noise itself offered camouflage, Rebecca would move a foot or two
closer to the cane.

Between Miss Davenport and the cane was a paddock
full of brown stubble and dust and hockey sticks *where
ignorant armies clashed by* . . . well, where eleven local
girls vied with eleven from Cairns High in the regional
semi-finals. Boys wolf-whistled from the sidelines.
Boys leaned on their bikes and laid bets on the outcome
of the game. Boys lay on the grass for the very best view
of Dellis's panties.

Miss Davenport saw Rebecca reach the cane. For a
few seconds, Rebecca's hair was a black swatch against
the purple tassels of the ripening stalks, then the girl
disappeared.

Hazel had disappeared during the first ten minutes of
the match, but that was different. The methods were
different. Hazel had the spooky powers of a gecko
lizard. You could stumble across Hazel in the middle of
an empty paddock, sitting cross-legged on the ground,
as unobtrusive as grass. "Hazel!" you might say, dumbfounded. "How long have you . . .?" But because of
something in Hazel's eyes, you never quite finished your
question. And Hazel never answered you. She hardly
ever spoke at all. She had another name which nobody
could pronounce, though sometimes you heard it when
one of her younger siblings came for the lunch. (In

Hazel's family, the kids had to take turns; Hazel was the one who carried the much-creased brown bag and made the decisions.) *Joanna Goanna*, the boys called her, taunting.

Miss Davenport squinted and surveyed the entire paddock from the cane to the school buildings. It was quite possible that Hazel was there somewhere, watching the hockey game, willing them all to believe she was the magpie in the poinciana tree.

Rebecca had vanished.

Miss Davenport kept her eye on the magpie which looked right back and commanded: *Sleep, sleep, sleep, sleep* . . .

"The last of the Hapsburgs," Charlie said. "That's what people call them."

"Who?" Miss Davenport asked.

"Her parents. That girl's. The one you go on about."

"Rebecca Weiss?"

"Yeah. Her mum and her old man, one hundred percent bonkers. Joe Hawkins at the Commonwealth Bank started it. He sees them once a month, they're rich as Midas, got most of it stashed somewhere in their place up the Daintree, Joe reckons. Not in their bank account, that's for bloody certain. They got *investments* in Sydney and Brisbane, that's what Joe reckons. They bring Joe their piddling deposits once a month, a bloody joke, typical Ikey. The last of the Hapsburgs, Joe says, and it caught on. Whoever the hell the Hapsburgs were."

"Austro-Hungarian emperors," Miss Davenport said. "Rulers in Europe from the thirteenth century to the First World War."

"Yeah?" Charlie laughed. "Well, there you are. Bloody peculiar, that's all I know. Mind you, anything

you want to dream up, you can find up the Daintree. It's
a zoo up there." Charlie ticked off the fingers of his left
hand with the index finger of his right: "Crocs in the
Daintree itself, and in the rainforest, you name it: Japs
who've been lost since New Guinea, boat people, hip-
pies, paddocks of mary-j that stretch all the way up to
Torres Strait, greenies, Jesus freaks, Martians,
dinosaurs, and the last of the Hapsburgs in their castle."

"Castle?"

"Yeah. Well, good as." Charlie O'Hagan drained his
beer and signalled for another. "And I should know, I
been there once." He leaned back on the stuffed leather
banquette and laced his fingers behind his head. Lucia
Davenport noted the strain in the fabric of his trousers
when he did this: the creases, the protuberance, the welt
of muscle along the thigh. Charlie closed his eyes and
breathed deeply, and from off the top of his fresh-
tapped beer he blew the froth of that up-the-Daintree
circus.

"Two storeys high," Charlie said. "And I don't
mean it's got an under-the-house. I mean, two floors all
inside, the way they have in England. And the roof has
pointy things, castle things, whad'ya call em?"

"Spires?" she asked. "Minarets?"

"Minarets, yeah." Charlie opened his eyes and smiled
a slow smile. He drank a golden mouthful and let the
golden word and the liquid slip pleasurably together,
making a tour of his veins. "Minarets," he repeated, in
love with the sound of them, the idea of them. "Yeah,
minarets. That's what it's got. Twenty or thirty
sprouting out of the roof like bloody pawpaw shoots."

"Oh Charlie." She laughed, pushing a puddle of beer
across the table with one finger, accidentally brushing
his hand. "You and the blarney stone."

"They got more rooms than you could shake a stick at."

"How many rooms?"

"And servants," he said, rising to a warm and beery eloquence, "with velvet bloomers like your grandma used to wear."

None of this, alas, could be put in the letters to Ida. It would never do, it would be sheer lunacy, to submit Charlie to a reading by Ida. Charlie, alas, had a reading audience of one. But there, he was without fixed form or narrative limit; in secret genre, he flourished as extravagantly as climbing pandanus up the Daintree.

"And in a room smack in the middle of the mansion," Charlie elaborated, "in a bloody *wardrobe*, no windows, that old codger Weiss turns Daintree fungus into gold."

Charlie O'Hagan, Mossman cop, married man, father of a good Catholic brood (several of whom learned their EnglishFrenchHistoryGeography from Miss Davenport, high school arts teacher) met with Lucia as often as possible. Not in Mossman, needless to say. And not in Cairns, which would not have been any safer, bars having at least a thousand ears, especially where schoolteachers and policemen were concerned. No. Luckily Charlie had connections and they met offshore in the floating tourist hotel. They drifted as whim took them: Green Island, the outer reef, the Whitsunday Passage, wherever. They left no wake.

Miss Davenport leaned across the table in the dimly lit bar. "Do you mean he's an alchemist?" she asked. "Rebecca's father?"

"Yeah," Charlie said. "That's the word, I reckon. Makes this dynamite dope out of fungus, pure gold in Sydney. Got his private fleet of hippie runners, that's what we reckon. We turn a blind eye. But we'll bust things up quick as a wink if we ever have to.''

"But you *wouldn't*, Charlie, oh you wouldn't, would you? You can't believe a word of all that, it's just talk. And they're so shy, they're so harmless, and Rebecca's so . . . Anyway, you're not that kind of policeman.''

Charlie O'Hagan put down his beer and coughed. ''Yeah, well. Don't spread the word. Do me in, if they find out what a softie . . .'' He grabbed her hands, slopping beer on the table. Policeman and school teacher slid into collision on slick leather. Ignoring the waitress, Charlie O'Hagan sent his rough cop's tongue on a voyage inside Miss Davenport's mouth. ''I gotta get you into bed,'' he said. ''In the next five minutes, or else.''

Without coming up for air from the kiss, Charlie O'Hagan snapped his fingers, and the manager pulled up anchor. Four stars streaming, the hotel tacked into the wind, making for the steamy place where the Daintree spills into the sea.

The boys thought Rebecca was ugly, plainjane, a real dog, a praying mantis, a barbwire tangle of sticklimbs and sharp points, so of course Rebecca believed them. Miss Davenport thought she was striking in the manner of Virginia Woolf, the kind of girl whose gaunt cheekbones and deep eye sockets will become memorable — though perhaps not ever in Mossman.

On a certain Friday in the not-quite-so-wet part of the year, gangly Rebecca, who wrote unsettling English compositions modelled on Dostoevsky, hung about Miss Davenport's desk.

''My, uh, father and mother,'' she said in her oddly formal, oddly desperate way, ''wish to, uh, invite you . . .'' Shyness scrunched Rebecca's eyes tightly shut. "They, uh, told me I had to invite you for *shab-bas*."

Miss Davenport, not entirely precisely clear on the subject of *shabbas*, answered carefully. "When is that, Rebecca? *Shabbas?*"

"It's, uh, tonight," Rebecca said. "For tea."

Miss Davenport raised surprised eyebrows. She was touched. Rebecca, however, twisting the damp edge of her school uniform in her hands, gave every sign of hoping that her invitation would be turned down. Miss Davenport bit her lip, compassionate. The last of the Hapsburgs, Charlie whispered in her ear. She saw minarets. Curiosity, alas, overcame her.

"That would be lovely, absolutely lovely, Rebecca. I'd love to come." Rebecca's lashes fluttered across despairing eyes. "But how will we . . .?" Miss Davenport began to ask.

"On Fridays, uh . . . they, um, my parents drive down." During the week, Rebecca boarded at the Methodist parsonage next door to the school. "We have to, uh, be back by sundown. They'll be waiting for us, uh, at the Post Office."

He's like a goblin, Miss Davenport wrote to Ida. *So is the mother. And only alchemy could keep that car functioning. The drive takes an hour, and the forest starts smothering everything once you're fifteen minutes north of Mossman. It's like moving inside green yeast.*

There were no minarets.

There are two storeys, Lucia wrote to Ida. *But it's rather like a dollhouse, or a farmhouse in the Black Forest, and very beautifully made out of cabinet timbers. Mr Weiss built it himself, and the mother weaves tapestries on a loom. They take carvings and weavings to Kuranda and Cairns to sell. Poor as church-mice, I'd say. Hardly any furniture, but everything handmade and wonderful to touch. And everywhere, floor to ceiling, there are piles and piles of books. I've never seen so many books.*

At table, there were candles, and place settings for five.

"Rebecca," Mr Weiss said in his heavily accented voice. "Ask Leo if he will please come down and join us with our guest for *shabbas*."

Rebecca, expressionless, looked first at her mother, but her mother was ladling vegetable stew. She looked at her father. She twisted the hem of her skirt in her hands.

"Rebecca?" her father asked, his eyebrows raised.

Rebecca climbed the silky-oak staircase, trailing a hand up the banister. She disappeared for a full two minutes. Miss Davenport spoke warmly of Rebecca's writing.

"Yes, yes," Mr Weiss said, nodding. "In the beginning, God *spoke*. There was a word and it contained everything. Everything." He nodded and nodded, beaming at her. "The word," he said. "The word. We are grateful to you."

Rebecca came slowly downstairs. "Leo is unable to join us, Father," she said.

"Ah." Mr Weiss sighed and bowed his head. "But perhaps only to be expected, yes?"

Candles were lit, bread broken, wine drunk. Mr Weiss spoke of music and books, of Mendelssohn and Isaac Babel . . . Would Miss Davenport, perhaps, be teaching Babel's stories in the English class?

"Actually," Miss Davenport confessed, embarrassed, "to tell you the truth, I'm afraid I'm not familiar with . . . I haven't actually had the pleasure . . ."

"Yes, yes, *Red Cavalry* and *Tales of Odessa,* ah *there* was — as Babel called himself — the master of the genre of silence." Mr Weiss spoke of things not lost because the silence preserved them. He spoke of the words of silence and the silence of words. He talked with manic excitement and speed, as though he were some necessary counterpoint to the masters of silence.

Mrs Weiss did not speak at all.

"Rebecca," Mr Weiss said when the plates had been cleared, "will you ask Leo if he will play for us now? For our guest? The Mendelssohn, tell him, he cannot refuse us."

Rebecca did not look at Miss Davenport, but Miss Davenport watched Rebecca's face, in profile, floating upstairs at the top of her shoulders. It was like a mask, like a waxwork image of Rebecca.

They waited. Mr Weiss spoke of Mendelssohn, of silence, of darkness, of how all that mattered could be preserved if one got far enough from distracting noise and light. "Getting far enough away, that is the secret," he said, nodding, nodding. "Silence and darkness. Although such problems for the violin, poor Leo, *ach!* You have no idea of the problems, the rainforest, the heat, the moisture, *oi vay.*"

"Father," Rebecca said in a low voice, descending. "Leo says he will play, but he will not come downstairs."

"Ah, ah!" Mr Weiss raised his wineglass to the stairs. "He will play."

Mrs Weiss folded her hands in her lap and closed her eyes. Rebecca twisted her skirt in her fingers and studied the tablecloth. Mr Weiss began rocking gently backwards and forwards, eyes closed, a smile on his face. "Ah," he sighed blissfully. "Mendelssohn."

Miss Davenport heard the usual forest noises, the calls of nightbirds, the cicadas.

And then, she wrote to Ida, *I don't know how to explain this, but I heard it too. I definitely began to hear a violin. At first it was so faint that I thought I was hearing the echo of Mr Weiss's hope, but then it was Mendelssohn, unmistakably. The first movement of the violin concerto. When it ended, Mr Weiss was crying.*

Lucia did not mail this letter to Ida.

"Rebecca," Miss Davenport said, as they walked west, late the next Wednesday afternoon, on the road that led to the Mossman Gorge. Dust rose in little mushroom clouds around their sandals. "Who is Leo?"

"Dad's oldest son. He used to play in an orchestra." Rebecca looked at Miss Davenport and then away. "Second marriages. They both had other children but there was no one left. I was born out here. After . . . all that."

It was a three-mile walk through tunnels of cane in a swooning heat that dripped across the forehead and down the neck and gathered wetly in bodily creases. Then they would climb into the shadow of the Divide, where the gorge was full of deep green pools and falls and ferns.

Rebecca had been alarmed by the invitation. "What if someone sees?" she'd asked nervously. She was afraid of being called teacher's pet; she feared open spaces and long exposures. Lucia had had to wait for her half a mile along the road.

Lucia imagined what Rebecca might write in her diary: *She watches me all the time, and today she asked me to go swimming at the gorge. Help! Some of the girls think she's queer.*

Rebecca said: "I suppose you think we're crazy?"

"No, Rebecca, I don't."

Heat, cane, dust, steamfoghaze. It was like walking through dreams. Miss Davenport's voice came sleepily, drugged. "You'll win scholarships, Rebecca. To university. You'll escape from here."

Rebecca stopped then, turning, swaying a little in the haze. "But this is where we've escaped to," she said.

They walked. At the end of the road, just before the wet mouth of forest licked up unpaved grit and dust, the Reserve slouched against the mountain, a sorry place. Some Mister Government Man, well intentioned perhaps, had hacked clear a crater between forest and canefields, a pitiless saucer of red dust in which he had planted twenty fibro huts on low stumps. Men sat on the wooden steps, children chased each other in the compound.

"There's Hazel," Rebecca said.

"Where? Oh!" Miss Davenport waved and called. A hush and a stillness fell abruptly on the children playing tag. Thirty or more faces, the faces of men, women, and children, stared silently.

Hazel, barefoot but still wearing her school uniform, did not move.

"Hazel?" Miss Davenport called again, less certainly.

Hazel came forward slowly, her bare feet sending up dust signals, her eyes down.

"Hazel," Miss Davenport said. "Rebecca and I are going to swim at the gorge. Would you like to come with us?"

Hazel rubbed one bare foot against the other leg and studied the busy columns of bull-ants emerging from pockmarks in the earth near her feet. She touched the black juicy bulbs of an ant body with her big toe, and the three women watched a file break rank and follow its leader across the mound of Hazel's foot. Fifty ants later, Hazel looked from Miss Davenport to Rebecca

and back to Miss Davenport. Since the invitation was
not withdrawn, she bit her lip and giggled a little and put
a hand over her mouth to cover her shyness. "Okay,"
she said, from under her hand. She giggled again, and
blushed. She called something back over her shoulder
and flicked her hand in a curious way. It was as though
she had pulled a switch: noise began, the men looked
away, the children went back to play.

Miss Davenport the schoolteacher and her two pupils
left the bare saucer of the reserve and crossed the shade
line.

The change was abrupt. The light turned green, the
temperature dropped, webs of lawyer cane lay in wait.
Below the falls (they were only ten feet high, but
aggressive) the pool was as green as the matted canopy
above. Hazel tossed her tunic and blouse over a rock
and dived in, a shallow arc, from the bank. She was not
wearing underwear. Rebecca and Miss Davenport
registered this with mild shock.

The Methodist minister's wife, Lucia mentally wrote
to Ida, *donated the uniform and shoes. Hazel, no
doubt, would have been too shy to specify further
needs, and it would not have occurred to the minister's
wife, or any of us, for that matter* . . .

Rebecca took off her uniform and folded it neatly.

*Ribs like corrugations on mother's old wooden
washboard,* Miss Davenport saw herself writing. *So
painfully thin, I couldn't bear to look. For a moment,
Rebecca seemed to be assessing the disadvantages of
walking back into town with wet underwear, but then
she entered the water with tentative steps until only her
head was visible. Perhaps she could not quite subject
herself to open comparison with voluptuous Hazel.*

In the green pool the two heads floated with their
dark hair fanned about them: waterlilies on lily pads. A

languid steamy contentment suffused Miss Davenport. Back on the hockey field, in the sticky heat, she had thought only of coolness, water, the gorge. Rebecca had been an afterthought, an impulse: Hazel another impulse. But sometimes . . . *All manner of thing shall be well.* She saw the words in black floreate script on parchment. She smiled.

Green coolness, she had been thinking on the hockey field. The gorge, the falls, the pool.

She had not thought of the matter of clothes at all, how it complicated things. And now, after all, it was irrelevant again, for all manner of thing would be well.

Miss Davenport, with a careless rapture, took off all her clothes and walked into the water.

The pool, from dark subterranean places, was chilly, a shock to the body for whole minutes. Time must have passed, though the three women were not conscious of it. They did not speak, but they were aware of each other. Birds piped and flashed their colours, the falls kept up their subdued chatter.

This is where we have escaped to, Miss Davenport thought. One is safe in water.

One is helpless in water.

Afterwards, she could never understand how there was no warning, no transition. Just peace, and then chaos, the jarring laughter and catcalls, the five boys standing on boulders.

Joanna Goanna's tits! they whooped. *Cop those black tits! Plainjane hasn't got any tits, she's flat as a bat. Oh 'struth, cop that! You can see old Dried-up Davenport's pussy!*

The boys, Miss Davenport noted, were in an intense and spiritual state, a kind of sacrilegious ecstacy, leaping from boulder to boulder around the pool. Like kings of the wild, they stood high on the great black rock and pissed into the water. Then one of them, Ross O'Hagan, eldest son of the local policeman, an ordinary boy who sat at an ordinary desk in Miss Davenport's English class, that boy turned his back and pulled down his shorts and squatted. A turd emerged slowly and hung suspended from his hairy anus. It was long, amazingly long, making its celebrity appearance to a chanted count. One! the boys chanted. Two, three, four, five. . . .

Miss Davenport, Rebecca, and Hazel watched, mesmerised. The turd had attained the count of ten, a plumbline reaching for water. Eleven, twelve, thirteen . . . It detached itself at last and fell into the pool with a soft splash. Cheers went up, and more whoops of laughter, and then the boys were off like possums, flying from rock to rock. They scooped up the bundle of female clothing, and ran off.

Miss Davenport was able, for a moment, to think of the value her nylon panty would have as trophy: a relic almost, handed from boy to high-school boy until it passed into legend.

Water lapped at their shoulders. Polluted water. Hazel, inured to indignity perhaps, was the first to move. She clambered onto the boulder below the falls and let the water hammer her. Once she slipped, and fell back into the pool, and climbed out again; she submitted her body to the punitive shower.

But what comfort could Miss Davenport give to Rebecca whose face had put on its whitewax look-alike mask? How could she unsay the sentence that had been spoken, become an Anti-Circe? In her teacherly mind, she rehearsed possible spells: *This says more about the boys than it does about us.*

But it would not serve, she knew it. It might be true,

but it would not serve. That steaming fact, dropping stolidly into the pool, spoke a thick and dirty language. The acts of men, even when they are boys, Miss Davenport thought, are shouts that rip open the signs that try to contain them. We have no access to a language of such noisiness. Our voices are micemutter, silly whispers.

We will have to stay here in the pool forever, she thought. We are dead ends, the last of a line, masters of the genre of silence. We will have to invent a new alphabet of moss and water.

Hazel, wet and comfortably naked, walked out of the pool. Miss Davenport shook herself as a terrier does. We'll have to cover ourselves with something, she thought briskly. We'll have to walk back before it gets dark.

Uncle Seaborn

In all the photographs, Uncle Seaborn has his long strange hair tied back in a *queue*. It is soft as water, crinkly (one thinks of wavelets rippling back over sand), the colour of seaweed. In one daguerreotype, bending over the ingot sluice at the Mt Morgan mine, he is caught between his elements: gold, and the ocean which pulled at him. He is half-enveloped by steam — it comes off the bullion bricks as they hit the water — and the filaments of his seaweed hair lift and sway against the moist aurora of the furnace. A gleaming creature, barebacked and slick with sweat, he reaches in with wood-handled pincers, lifts, stacks the gold. Behind him (though the photograph does not, of course, show this), the Great Divide falls away to the coastal plain, and the wet tendrils of hair drip down ravines of muscle and bone, of eucalypt scrub, of Fitzroy River silt, making their way to the Pacific. It sucked at him ceaselessly, the ocean.

There were far more photographs than Clem had expected: his mother had hoarded them, his father had

catalogued and labelled. Clem sifted the past, over-
come. In every drawer: Mt Morgan, Rockhampton,
Emu Park, Yeppoon, his own life and those of his
forebears mapped and milestoned; his father smiling in
the Post Office, his father tapping out morse code; his
parents' sepia wedding. And from further back: his
mother with Seaborn at the old mine, beside a dray, on
the headland at Emu Park, on the beach, two strange-
lings, two children in Edwardian clothes, waiting hand-
in-hand for disaster.

And here were frail letters of condolence from
England; along the creases, they fell apart like ash. Here
was a bundle . . . ah, compunction . . . here was every
letter Clem had sent home for thirty-five years,
numbered, dated, indexed in his father's neat hand: a
slim packet, reproachfully slim. There were other things
too: lace collars, cuff links, pearl studs, gloves that but-
toned from wrist to elbow, linen handkerchiefs with
crocheted edges. Not to mention the shells, starfish,
sand dollars, cuttlefish, conches. His mother had had a
fetish for shells. His father had kept everything,
everything, and had gone on adding, believing that the
past conferred meaning.

But what had they meant, these unobserved working-
class lives?

When Clem found the little copy of Ruskin's *Sesame
and Lilies* (its vellum cover and tissue pages as
vulnerable, as gentle, as his mother), loss hit him with
the thump of a rogue breaker. He could hear his father
reading Ruskin aloud: the rough Australian voice, the
yearning for graciousness, for significance, for the
Imprimateur of the Mother Country where civilisation
happened. Without warning, a sobbing distress visited
Clem, as a sudden storm at sea swamps a boat.

Connect, connect. Urgently, he fumbled his way

through multiple digits and international operators to speak to his wife and children in Canada. They offered comfort, they spoke soothing words, but it seemed to him the entire intervening ocean was on the line, he could hear the constant shush of interference. *This was how my mother felt,* he grieved, *and my grandmother before her*.

But no. In sober honesty, no. This was a pale shadow of their terrible isolation.

"Where are you?" his wife asked. Her voice was faint as the tide going out.

"Rockhampton," he said. "The old house. I'm still sorting through their things." He wanted to say: It's like combing the sand at Emu Park for leftover mines. The past is blowing up in my face. "You know what hoarders they were."

"We miss you," his wife and children said. "We love you."

"I can't hear you," he panicked. The surf of static again, the whispering, hissing, wave-washing, word-washing, the line going dead. The tyranny of distance, he thought. The ocean wins every time.

In the next drawer he found Uncle Seaborn's gold half-sovereign and felt elation, then fear, then elation.

Clem sits where the Tropic of Capricorn slices through Queensland sand, and studies the coin. Queen Victoria stares at his thumb, not amused. She intones historical facts: good currency of the realm, minted 1884 in the thirty-seventh year of our reign, and not originally intended for dubious use as a *bon voyage* charm to the underside of the world when, in February 1893, at Tilbury Docks, said coin was placed in the hand of an infant in its mother's arms.

For good luck, it is reported that Clem's great-grandparents said at the time. Gold finds gold, they hinted. It draws itself to itself.

And Clem's grandfather, stern Methodist, informed his wife's parents that it was no earthly treasure the emigrants sought in Australia. "We lay up for ourselves," he said — and frowned as his infant son's fingers curled around Mammon — *"we lay up for ourselves treasures in heaven where neither moth nor rust doth corrupt. For where your treasure is there shall your heart be also."*

The Lord bless thee and keep thee, Clem's great-grandparents said, subdued.

They kept the letter that their daughter mailed from Rockhampton to Birmingham in July 1893. They and their non-nomadic children and their children's children kept it. Half a century later, a second cousin twice removed sent it back to Queensland. *Historical curio,* he wrote. *Found it in a box after dad died. Thought it would mean more to you than to us.* The letter's original voyage to England took four months; its return trip took eight days. In Clem's father's cataloguing hand, the letter is indexed and labelled: *Birth of Seaborn.*

My beloved parents:

I have such sad news to impart, which I cannot do without weeping again so that it is scarcely possible to see what I write. We have been safely arrived these six weeks, but I have been ill of a fever and grief, and am even now scarcely able . . .

Poor little Alfred died when we were ten weeks at sea. It is crossing the equator, the ship's doctor says.

We sang Abide with Me and the Reverend Watson read Suffer the little children from scripture, but I cannot speak of the feelings which overwhelmed me when the waters closed over my little Alfred's body . . .

The Lord taketh away and the Lord giveth, Thomas says. In the eleventh week, my pains came upon me early and I was safely delivered of a second son by the ship's doctor. We have called him Seaborn. The sea taketh and giveth. The sea is God's handmaid, Thomas says. At the christening, which the Reverend Watson was obliged to conduct at my bedside, I placed in Seaborn's hand the coin that you gave to little Alfred, which much displeased Thomas. He says render unto Caesar the things which are Caesar's and to God the things which are God's.

Clem holds the coin against his ear and hears the surf; or it could be the tides of his grandmother's weeping. She sits with his mother on the rocks and both of them stare at the sea. *For where your treasure is*, they murmur, *there shall your heart be also.*

Clem rubs the worn edge of the coin and Uncle Seaborn billows forth with a vapour of words in his mouth. *What is your wish?* he whispers.

I want to dream your dreams, Clem says.

Ahh . . . Words crest and foam on Seaborn's breath. *Every night I went back, I went home.*

Seaborn waited every night for that moment when the moon slipped between the Mt Morgan minehead and the stringy-barks, that moment when his room filled with water. If he lay propped on one elbow he could watch it coming, a tidal welling that moved back up through the Fitzroy delta, lapped Mt Archer, drowned the valley in between, washed the Mt Morgan scarp, and filled his room with green light. *Seaborn, Seaborn,* a voice would call as creatures of the deep call each other. It was a low and maddening sound, unbearably plaintive. Seaborn's arms would lift themselves and sway in the thick green light, he would dreamswim into the lonely desiring of his brother Alfred. Every night they embraced. They played together. Water was their natural element, even as a child Seaborn knew it. At night, his gills fluttered and sucked, the webbing appeared between his toes. When he spread his fingers, there were skeins of skin thinner than silk that reached to the second knuckle.

Awake, he could not be kept from pools, from creeks, from rivers. He swam like a fish, though his mother was afflicted with nightmares in which staghorn coral gutted him and angelfish darted through his hair. Seaborn's father sweated over ingots and furnace, but once a year the family made the daylong horse-and-dray journey down the mountain to Rockhampton, an odyssey of twenty-four miles. They spent two days in the city and then travelled by train another thirty miles to the beach. Seaborn's mother never let him out of her sight, though her son took to the ocean as if he had flippers and gills. When they had to leave, he threw tantrums.

Grace was born with her mother's fear of the water in her blood. She arrived at the century's tide-turn, late in 1899, on a night of cyclonic rains, a night when the Fitzroy lost track of its banks. Chaos. Delirium. *Water, water*, Grace's mother gasped, but then refused to drink and recoiled from fluids in terror. Water swallows my babies, she wept.

For the lying-in, the family had come down to Rockhampton, but even so the doctor who rowed and rowed from concussions to birthings was not there to tend the dehydrated fever, not in time for the coming of Grace. Seaborn and Alfred, awash in the flooding night, felt the shock of birth-cries like sonic pain on the underside of their fins. Their mother bent over her contractions, moaning, as a diver jackknifes with the bends. *It is a judgment*, their father said. His voice reached them like the thunder of a great whale and they clung to each other. But by morning, a girl child was born. *By the grace of God,* their father said.

Seaborn and Alfred, who were six and seven years old, adored her. Every night they brought treasures: shells, coral, driftwood, seaweed as fine as mermaid's hair. They placed them at her feet where she waited, fearful, above the high water line.

Grace hoarded their gifts. As she grew older, every windowsill, every shelf, the surface of her dresser, her drawers, all were crowded with shells and starfish and branches of coral. She had a fetish for things from the sea, but she never set foot in the water. Of docks, jetties, boats, and beaches, she had an unnatural dread. Each year, when the family made its annual trip down the mountain, Grace sat with her mother on the rocks at a very considerable distance from the scalloped line of foam. Grace and her mother kept their eyes fixed on Seaborn's dolphin body as though even so much as a blink in their constant attention might spell disaster. Sometimes — such is the trickster effect of sun on water — they seemed to see two of him, Seaborn and a mirage swimmer, a *doppelgänger*. Then Seaborn's mother would put her head in her hands and weep.

When Seaborn enlisted in 1914, the family moved down the mountain and into the city. Grace kept Seaborn's photograph beside her bed. She adored him. She kept his gold half-sovereign (he had given it to her for safekeeping) under her pillow. When she held it against her ear, she could hear his troopship pushing through the Dardanelles. She believed that when she held it against her heart, he was safe. Seaborn's mother trusted to ceaseless prayer, his father said that all was as God disposed.

Torpedoes, submarines, Turkish shells, they all courted Seaborn, but he led a charmed life, people said. The war came to an end, as all things do. There was a party. There were banners and flags in Rockhampton, there was movement at the station (a festive riot, to be more precise), and there was Seaborn, along with five other Rockhampton boys, rolling in on their sea-legs, brass buttons flashing, something strong and fermented on their breaths. Grace remembered. She remembered the music, the laughter, the loud talk. She remembered Seaborn's whiskery kiss, and she remembered the moment when she put the gold half-sovereign back in his hand. He lifted her up then, hugging her, swinging her round until she was giddy, laughing something into her ear: "I saw him out there, behind the ship." "Saw who?" she asked. But he only laughed harder.

There was something disturbing in his laughter, something . . .? She could not find a word for it. She could only think of a king tide coming in, the way nothing can stop it.

And later, when he was very drunk, she heard him say something to their mother in the kitchen. "I saw Alfred, Mum, when we were crossing the equator."

Clem has this memory: he is seven; he and his father are slick with water and salt; they run along the sand at Yeppoon. Beyond the sand, under the pine tree, his mother Grace and his sisters spread the picnic cloth, set out the thermos, the cups, the egg sandwiches.

"Why won't Mum ever go in the water?" Clem asks.

"She's afraid of it, she always has been. Because of Uncle Seaborn, I reckon. He drowned before you were born."

"How'd he drown, Dad?"

"A riptide, the current from Ross Creek. You can see it." Clem's father points to the ribbon of pale water within the blue. "It was strange though, he was such a strong swimmer. Your mother thought he was waving, and waved back. He'd only been home from the war a few months."

Clem has another memory: he is eight now? nine? His mother sits by the rocks that are higher than the high tide line. Clem runs from the water, gleaming, and sits beside her. "What are you staring at, Mum?"

She startles. She has her hand in the pocket of her skirt, her fingers are always playing with something hidden. "What's in your pocket, Mum?"

She smiles at him, but strangely, as though she is smiling in her sleep. She takes the gold coin out and holds it against Clem's ear. "What do you hear?" she asks him.

The shell game. "I can hear the sea," Clem says.

"What else?" She puts her cheek against his. "Can't you hear anything else?"

Clem thinks. The gulls wheel and screech above him. "I hear shrieks," he says.

He cannot forget the way she flinches, the look in her eyes. "No," she says, shivering. "No. Not shrieks. It's the way they call to each other."

Clem has always lived by water.

Alone on the beach in Central Queensland, chill July and chiller mid-life, he strokes the pine tree where his mother used to spread the picnic cloth, he climbs the rocks that he and his father climbed, he walks the cliff path where his sisters loved to walk. He stands on the headland and looks out at the islands, every one of which he can name. He wishes his wife and children were with him. He rubs the coin in his pocket.

Between the headland and Pelican Island, something moves in the water. A shape. Two shapes. Small fishing boats? Sharks perhaps? Dolphins?

Something barrels into Clem, a wave of excitement. He races crazily down to the beach, rips off his clothes, drops them into a quick neat heap on the sand, tucks Uncle Seaborn's half-sovereign carefully into the toe of one shoe, and rushes into the water. After the first wintery shock of the cold, a manic pleasure comes. He swims strongly, stroke after stroke, his old Australian crawl, toward the twin shapes. He laughs as he swims, he is flooded with a pure intense joy.

I have come home, he thinks. I am where I belong.

The Second Coming of Come-by-Chance

In the sixty-fourth month of the tribulation, just five weeks before the drought finally broke, people began driving out from Townsville and Ayr and Home Hill, from Charters Towers and Collinsville, and from any number of smaller salt-of-North-Queensland towns: Thalanga, Mungunburra, Millaroo, Mingela. The Flinders Highway was thick with four-wheel drives, the air with dust. Afterwards, newspapers remembered that there had been a curious sense of festivity about, a sort of overwrought camaraderie, the kind that comes in the wake of cyclones, earthquakes, bush fires. Post-traumatic hysteria, the articles said. Old men had visions, revenants appeared in the pubs, crackpots wrote to newspapers, children concocted secret ways of sucking juice from rocks and of finding the underground channels where the rivers had fled.

All this was mere prelude. It was Tom Kelly and Davy Cobb, unlikely angels of the apocalypse, who ushered in what the Brisbane papers dubbed a "Flight into Egypt" and the *Sydney Morning Herald*, predictably supercilious, headlined as "Latter Day Madness in Queensland". (Perhaps it is unnecessary, from this retrospective distance, and after so much analysis of the psychological effects of the drought, to note that those who live in the cities of the coastal plain, while not unaffected by years of water restrictions, are unlikely to be aware of the intensity of the inland thirst for something, for *anything*, to happen.) In any case, in the beginning it was just a trickle. Perhaps, that first weekend, only sixty people drove out to the dwindling Burdekin Dam to watch the reappearance of Come-by-Chance, for the tip of the Anglican steeple had been sighted by the two boys fishing in their homemade boat.

Sighted? *Bumped into* would be more accurate. Young Tom Kelly had laced a worm around his hook and cast his line. At the oars, Davy Cobb felt a jolt. What Tom hooked was the copper cross, green as verdigris, sticking out of the water like the index finger of God, potent, invisible (at least until the moment of reckoning). The faster Tom reeled in his catch, the swifter the little boat skimmed toward its ramming. Both boys went into the water like steeplejacks on the toss. This was a week before Christmas, and the momentum of Tom Kelly's unpremeditated dive was later likened by the Bishop of North Queensland to the downward swoop of the Incarnation. Tom claimed he looked through the rose window and saw a phosphorescent glow, then kept plummeting to the soft Gothic arch. The nave was full of green radiance.

"It was like there was sump'n *pullin'* me," he said. "I couldn't turn, I thought me lungs were gonna bust. Then I saw this kinda light, this kinda I dunno, like a million green parakeets' wings or sump'n, and then this *blaze* like a double-bunger star, it bloody well bursts inside me head. And next thing I know, Davy's thumpin' water outta me on the bank."

"An epiphany," the Bishop of North Queensland said. (It was the last Sunday in Advent.) But the pastor of the Gospel Hall in Mingela, the closest town to

Come-by-Chance, thundered darkly: "And in those days there shall be signs and portents, for He shall come as a fire descending . . ."

It is reasonably safe to assume that the *Sydney Morning Herald* would not have mentioned this spiritual event had it not been for the impending election and the clear correlation between water levels in the Burdekin Dam and political chaos in Queensland. The drought, it will be recalled, at first confined to that arid crescent between Townsville and Mt Isa, had spread like a virus. By the time of Tom Kelly's appearance on the front page of the tabloids, there were bush fires all the way to the Dandenongs and the Adelaide Hills. This "Queensland drift" seemed ominous, even to secular minds.

Addressing himself primarily to the political issues, a Sydney pundit commented, in passing, on the fishing story. Where else but in Queensland? he asked. Pressed by his interviewer to respond to a tabloid headline ("Christmas vision saves boy's life"), he spoke of the effects of shock and water-pressure and diminution of oxygen and concomitant hallucinatory indications such as the kind of aura that accompanies migraine or near-drowning, but no one in central or north Queensland watched this show. Indeed, even in Sydney and Melbourne, those infallible Geiger-counters of truth, many chose to ignore common sense. For what raconteur in the pub, what politician, what preacher, could resist Tom Kelly's aurora and the resurrection of Come-by-Chance?

"And there shall be famines," bishops and gospel firebrands read as with one voice. "And pestilences, and earthquakes in divers places. For then shall be great tribulation . . ." On exegesis, however, the divines parted ways, and quite contradictory moral and political

interpretations — not to mention voting admonitions —
were brought to bear. It was only in the actual scriptural
words of warning that they spoke as one again: "And
except those days should be shortened, there should no
flesh be saved: but for the elect's sake those days shall
be shortened."

A swelling group of the elect began to gather for vigil
and prayer and competitive political pamphleteering at
the ever-lower waterline of the dam. A week after the
fishing incident, the whole cross of St Stephen Martyr
was visible and a foot of steeple tiles below; in the
second week, the belltower of the Catholic church
appeared; in the third, the Post Office clock. Word
spread along the stock routes and talk-show arteries,
and via the pages that come round fish and chips. The
elect were joined by the curious, the bored, the Sydney
and Melbourne reporters, the television cameras, the
signs-and-portents groupies. A camp was set up.

"What come ye out for to see?" the Mingela pastor,
distributing tracts, asked through a megaphone. *Ahh,
knock it off*, people said, but not too savagely. Long
droughts of continental proportions induce nervous
piety in many breasts — though not in all. Around the
country, bookies also set up shop and punters laid bets
on the next building to resurrect itself. Daily the odds
were published on the likelihood of there still being
skeletons anchored to the stools in the bar, because
many people now recalled tales of Come-by-Chancers
who had refused to leave town.

The "flight into Egypt" became a veritable exodus,
and the *Sydney Morning Herald* ran a full weekend
feature in which the word "mirage" was frequently
mentioned. In Melbourne, the *Age* went as far as a
reference to "collective hysteria". This was due to the
curious fact that while everyone at the site, including

visiting reporters, could clearly see the re-emergent town, no trace of it showed up in photographs. The Logos Foundation issued a statement to the press: *Faith is the substance of things hoped for, the evidence of things not seen.* Only the pure in heart, it was implied, can witness the unblemished city of God. Come-by-Chance became symbol and rallying cry for a lost way of life, a simpler cleaner time, which each political party vowed to restore.

In the capital cities, editors were deluged with letters. No one could have predicted the number of people still living who had visited, or had relatives in, or had themselves inhabited the town of Come-by-Chance before it went under the dam. By one newspaper's count, the population had been a quarter of a million just prior to inundation, though the town had boasted only three churches, a post office, seven pubs, a one-teacher school, a police station (with two constables assigned) and a handful of shops and houses. There was considerable divergence of opinion on the erstwhile economic base. Sheep, most claimed. Opal prospecting, others contended. Tall stories, suggested the literary editor of the *Australian*, a man noted for his scepticism and wit. He alluded to Ern Malley and the whole issue of the literary hoax. He quoted Banjo Paterson, and left readers to draw their own conclusions:

*But my languid mood forsook me, when I found a
    name that took me;*
*Quite by chance I came across it — "Come-by-
    Chance" was what I read;*
*No location was assigned it, not a thing to help one
    find it,*
*Just an N which stood for northward, and the rest
    was all unsaid . . .*

> *But I fear, and more's the pity, that there's really*
>   *no such city,*
> *For there's not a man can find it of the shrewdest*
>   *folk I know;*
> *"Come-by-Chance", be sure it never means a land*
>   *of fierce endeavour —*
> *It is just the careless country where the dreamers*
>   *only go.*

Or where the victims of nightmares are trapped,
thought Mrs Adeline Capper. *And they can never leave.*

Adeline Capper dreaded the newspapers and read them
with a compulsive doomed fascination. She had always
known there was no way of expunging the past. One
could flee it, drown it, bury it, tear up the newsprint
record, but it went on skulking around today. It was
always *there*. Inside one. *Here.*

She was twenty then, sixty now, but twenty was as
close as her skin.

It is the doing nothing that is intolerable, she thought.
The fact that there is nothing to be done.

From her brown garden on the south side of
Townsville, she watched the trekkers herding down the
highway and out to the dam. A hot wind blew. Her
bougainvillea made a dead parchment sound against the
fence. Like a sleepwalker, she got into her car and
followed the columns of dust.

A settlement — a tent city — had sprung up: trailers,
kombi vans, canvas of all shapes and sizes, camp fires,
styrofoam iceboxes full of beer. People told jokes and
sang songs. There was raucous laughter, catcalls as
Adeline Capper moved among them. Was she twenty or
sixty? Night was such a dangerous time. *Hey, grandma!*
someone called. *Wanna cuppa?*

"Hey, didn't mean to give you such a scare," a young man said, apologetic. "Here. Have a cuppa tea."

She took it, shivering in the dry evening heat. Her teeth chattered.

"You all right?" the young man's wife asked, concerned.

They always asked that, but no one wanted to know the true answer. No one ever wanted to know that. She couldn't remember how far the reserve was from here, how far she had walked.

"See?" the young wife asked. She held out a wooden plaque, bleached colourless, soft to the touch. But you could still make out the carved indentation: XXXX.

"Four-X, the Queensland beer," the young man laughed. "A true-blue bit'v history. She was a bugger to rip off the wall, but."

"Brian dived," his wife said proudly. "You wouldn't believe what people are bringing up."

Oh, Adeline could well believe. And how soon would someone surface with her first teaching year? Who would wave it aloft? It was written in stone down there somewhere. Everywhere.

It was, it *is*, loud in the air.

"Where've you been, Adeline?" Sergeant Hobson had crooned, *croons,* pulling up beside her in the car. (Big Bob is what everyone calls him. She teaches his daughter in the one-teacher school.) He leans out and sings in her ear: "Oh where have you *been,* Adel-*een*?"

And she laughs, and Constable Terry Wilkes in the passenger seat laughs too. And they stand there in the moonlight on the dirt road winding into town from the reserve. "I've been visiting some of my school kids," she says. "The ones that live out . . . uh, the Chillagong ones."

"The boongs, you mean?"

Boongs. Abos. Everyone says it. It strikes her as terribly rude, but she doesn't want to offend, doesn't want to appear stuck-up, doesn't want to sound like the smart-alec who just arrived from Brisbane. "Yeah," she says.

"Bit late, innit?" Big Bob asks. "To be walking back into town."

"Yeah, I reckon." She laughs nervously. (She'd been terrified, as a matter of fact; and so relieved when the police car pulled up.) She'd thrown them into total confusion back there, Hazel, Evangeline, Joshua, their mothers and fathers, walking the three miles out after school. It isn't what anyone does, goes to Chillagong, she can see that now. "I got invited to stay for dinner." (Though she thinks they hadn't known what else to do, and nor had she; and the minute she'd accepted, she'd realised they hadn't expected her to. Perhaps hadn't wanted her to.)

"For *dinner*, well, stone the crows!" Big Bob and Constable Terry roar with laughter. "Kangaroo rat and witchetty grubs, ya like them, do ya?"

"Oh no," she shudders. In fact, she doesn't know what it was she ate. Some kind of stew.

"Well, get in then." Big Bob lumbers out and puts an arm around her shoulders. "We'll drive you back home." He presses his big fat lips against her neck and his beery breath hits her like a fist. "Can't have the little lady-teacher from Brisbane on her own in the bush at night." He strokes her hair protectively, and the front of her dress, accidentally pressing her breasts. She's a bit embarrassed, but they are the police, after all. She's between the two men on the Holden's bench-seat and feels safe.

"Adeline's been having a little night life with the

boongs," Big Bob tells Constable Terry. "She likes those big fat witchetty grubs."

"Big fat witchetty grubs," Terry sings. "Oh Adeleen, our village queen, she loves those big fat witchetty grubs."

"No, no," she protests laughing, but Big Bob joins in, and they sing and sway and laugh in the dark, and after a while she sings along: "I love those big fat witchetty grubs."

"She loves those big black witchetty grubs," sings Constable Terry.

Both men laugh so much that the car slews onto the shoulder and back, then off the road again. She's nervous now. She thinks they are both quite drunk.

"You think they're better?" Big Bob demands. "The big black juicy ones?"

She doesn't know what to answer. "Where are we going?" she asks, alarmed.

There's a blur, both car doors opening, a blank.

What she remembers: spiky grass and ants against her skin, and words marching in ranks through her head. *I don't believe this, I don't believe it, it doesn't make sense, it isn't happening.* And then the next day (she must have slept, or been unconscious, whatever), the next day: blood, bruises, and no clothes. No sign of her clothes. And diarrhoea, the worst, the most humiliating thing.

But she can remember only grass and ants and the shapes of words. The words themselves are jagged, they hurt her skin. Fog comes and goes. A search party shouts, she hunches herself up, ashamed, ashamed. She doesn't want to be found. The pain from moving is so great that she blacks out.

"Christ!" Big Bob has tears in his eyes. He covers her with a blanket. The picture in the newspaper shows him cradling her in his arms. "We found her clothes on the reserve," Big Bob tells the reporter. "The animals won't get away with it, I can promise you that."

Days come and go. She's teaching again, it seems. The children stare and whisper, the reserve kids don't come any more. She cannot look at Margaret, Big Bob's daughter. When she walks into the general store, people fall silent. "Poor Addie," they murmur, as though she has a terminal disease. "At least the bastards are in gaol," someone says. She stares, puzzled; there is something just out of reach, but only words rattle in her head like small change in an empty tin can. She has a nightmare, and in the morning she forces herself to read the papers that have stacked themselves up, unopened. She sees Joshua's father, Evangeline's father, in handcuffs. *We didn't do it, boss. We dunno how her clothes . . .*
A fever descends.

"Benevolent reasons" is what the transfer slip from the Education Department says. She lies awake all the last night, afraid. Wouldn't it be better, she begs herself, more sensible, to say nothing? Reasons for saying nothing marshal themselves in ranks, they file through her head all night. *Please*, her body begs. I have no choice, she tells it. I have to.
Morning. Two blocks to the police station, bodily panic, retreat. It takes her until the third attempt, and then Sergeant Big Bob Hobson and Constable Terry Wilkes greet her effusively. They take her into their office, they give her tea and a biscuit. "We're glad to see you up and about again," they say. "Glad to see you looking so well."

Her hands are sweating, her knees are weak, her throat dry.

"I am going to tell," she says. The noise each word makes as it falls on the floor is deafening.

They look at her blandly, innocent-eyed. "Tell what?" they ask.

Tell what? She feels dizzy, there is no bottom to this fall. She thinks: I will never know for sure again if night is night or day is day, what is dream or not-dream.

It would help, they told her at the hospital, to be a thousand miles away for a while. It would help, they said, to be somewhere where not a soul knew her. She took a year's leave, and went to Melbourne.

People were kind. At dinner parties in terrace houses they said to her, Of course Queensland gets the kind of government it deserves do you like the linguini? the salmon? in Brisbane we thought the food perfectly *ghastly* we do congratulate you on leaving, oh the Queensland police, the Aboriginal problem, no awareness at all, and Namatjira's tonal effects are *exquisite*, there was a black tie opening and we were simply overwhelmed *overwhelmed*, Aboriginal art's the going thing now a fantastic investment and I myself have a poem of social protest, a very *meaningful* people were kind enough a very socially aware in the *Age* will you have more champagne? you've come out of the wilderness, they said.

She was mute. The same hollow alphabet. No. Hollower. She could not acquire the knack of words that floated so weightlessly. She fled back to Queensland. She dreamed of alphabets that sent down deep webbing roots.

*　　*　　*

At dawn on the Burdekin banks (is she sixty or twenty?) she watches the foraging parties. Swimmers, dinghies, fights, whoops of delight. She huddles, not wanting to be found. Whole doors are coming up, chairs, verandah spindles, stovepipes, crosses, bits of clapboard, signs, signposts, there's a black market trade in souvenirs. At a trestle table, t-shirts are selling like hot cakes: *I was there for the Second Coming of Come-by-Chance.*

Adeline sits hugging herself, shivering in the fierce morning heat. Two gangs are fighting over the clock face from the Post Office tower, and a reporter in a frenzy of picture-taking swears irritably as he runs out of film. Rewind, unload, *rip* (the velcro carry-case), *rip* (the Kodak pack), *rip* (the foil covering). *"Shit!"* He tosses packet and foil over his shoulder. He is not an ordinary reporter. He has literary sensibilities and does these things, these projects, as a cultural enterprise, a refined monitoring of the pulse of the nation. He shakes his head at Adeline in disbelief. "I don't believe this. Bloody animals, a pack of hooligan looters." He gives off a kind of jubilation of disgust. "No one's going to *believe* this in Melbourne."

"No. No one ever believes." Nevertheless, that does not absolve . . . . She takes a deep breath. "I would like to set the record straight."

"Yeah, who wouldn't?" He's got the clock face and a bloodied forehead in focus, he's shooting like crazy.

"Capper is not my real name, I was never married, I am Adeline Crick."

"Yeah?"

"I want to tell you what really happened."

Christ, not another one. Any direction you point your lens. And she's got the DTs, the old soak, she's only worth one shot.

Adeline's words are heavy, their roots go down below the Burdekin, her clumsy tongue trips on them, she has to speak with the care of those who have had a stroke. She says: "I have the blood of innocent men on my hands."

"Oh," he says. "Right."

"At times one has to ask oneself," he wrote in a photo-essay that was given prominent space in the *Age*, "if Queensland is our own Gothic invention, a kind of morality play, the Bosch canvas of the Australian psyche, a sort of perpetual *memento mori* that points to the frailty of the skein of civilisation reaching out so tentatively from our southern cities.

"To return to Sydney or Melbourne and write of the primitive violence, the yobbo mentality, the mystics, the pathetic old women generating lurid and gratuitous confessions, the general sense of mass hallucination . . . to speak of this is to risk charges of sensationalism. And indeed, after mere days back in the real world, one has the sense of emerging from a drugged and aberrant condition.

"One has to ask oneself: Does Queensland actually exist?

"And one has to conclude: I think not.

"Queensland is a primitive state of mind from which the great majority of us, mercifully, have long since evolved. And Come-by-Chance is a dream within a nightmare, the hysteric's utopia, the city of Robespierre, Stalin, Jim Jones, the vision of purity from which history recoils.

"Come-by-Chance, we who are sane dilute you."

Yes, he'd done that rather well. Seen the essence of things, touched the depths, but kept the tone right. Words were his business, and if he often caught himself being plangent and acute, well, it was a forgivable sin. He was tempted to add a rider explaining how his work should be read, how his words should be picked up one by one like stones from the bank of an enchanted creek. But he would save that for another time.

When the drought broke with the series of maverick cyclones we all remember, there was flash flooding throughout central and southern Queensland. At the tent city on the Burdekin Dam, winds hurling themselves down from the Gulf at unprecedented inland speeds caused death and mayhem. Police estimated as many as forty people drowned. Cars were marooned on the Flinders Highway for days, army ducks were still rescuing stranded survivors weeks later. In both coastal and inland cities, powerline disasters, the uprooting of trees, and the collapse of buildings in the gale-force winds brought the region's death toll to over one hundred.

In Melbourne and Sydney, where water restrictions were at last lifted to everyone's immense relief, people read of the Queensland floods and shook their heads. If it's not one thing, it's another, they said.

I Saw Three Ships

Three ships came up out of the Pacific onto Collaroy Beach. Not ships exactly, though he had watched them sail out of the haze where North Head was, and past Long Reef. When he saw them turn shoreward and bear down on his fishing post — a folding chair in a pocket of cold winter sand — he thought he had finally (so many years after the event) gone mad; then he thought that the three pilots had.

The ships had a bead on him.

He was reeling in his past, what a catch. It figures, he thought. The whole wheeling world comes back to where it started, there's no help for it. He always knew he'd have to pay before the end.

At least this would lure the girl, and yes here she was coming down out of her concrete sky again. "Tenth floor," she'd answered yesterday. "I can see the seminary tower at Manly." He thought that was probably a lie, with all of Dee Why in between, but he knew about needing to believe in nice fictions. She'd have her reasons. *Interloper*, he'd thought irritably, just a week ago — he should have been able, in July, to count on the beach being his — but as day after day she had ignored him so completely, he'd felt challenged.

"You must be from down south," he'd said.

She'd looked surprised. "Well . . . yes, originally. I was born in Melbourne."

"I mean, from down south in Sydney." She'd laughed, startled, her eyebrows darting upwards like birds. He said: "It's only hardy locals and a few city weirdos who come to the beach in July."

"Oh." She had not bothered to stop and be social. She had just gone on walking towards the rocks.

You had to wonder about a young woman alone.

Now she was letting the wavelets curl around her ankles, shading her eyes, staring out at the kamikaze ships.

"I don't believe in them either," he joked into the wind, but as usual she failed to respond.

When the ships splashed into the shallows they sprouted wheels and clambered out of the water, rasping, snorting, noisier than a bevy of beached whales. Jesus, he thought. What you reel in if you live too long! The same fucking army ducks he'd seen parading out of New Guinea and into the sea. The shivers hit him. He was too bloody old for this, too bloody old to fish in July, sitting still till he caught his death. His reel jammed, he had to throw down the rod half tangled. While he folded his chair, all thumbs, the army ducks wheeled and roared, a mating game of rhinoceros.

"Catch anything, grandpa?" called a kid — a mere boy — in khaki. You would have been sushi by now, mate, the old man muttered. Men were dropping over the tailgates like gravel on the spill, some sort of manoeuvre, what a farce, what a blooming picnic, a game with museum pieces. He could just imagine: hunt the nuclear missile, race you to the fallout shelter. The men wore yellow oilskins, for god's sake, over their uniforms. There was probably a waterproof fridge stuffed tight with beers in the cabin.

A young officer dropped to the sand like a god; and
landed face to face with the girl.

Some things at least never changed.

The old man's shivers were bad. The chair, resisting
his attempts to fold it, took a savage bite out of one
hand. Jesus, he swore, extricating his fingers and sucking them. As he stumbled up the beach with his gear, he
could see the young officer making his moves: an ac-
cidental lurching in the wet sand, collision with a thigh,
a necessary clutch to steady himself. But the girl tossed
her head and the long single braid that hung down her
back twitched free like the tail of a haughty filly.

The old man laughed through his shivers: You'll
never get anywhere with that one. A nun in the making,
I can smell them.

It was too early for the pub.

At the bottle shop, a girl with green streaks in her hair
eyed him sharply. "You got the DT's, mate?"

He frowned, giving her his look of offended dignity.

"Aren't you Old Gabe from down at the rooming
house?" She was watching him cautiously. "I'm not
allowed to sell if you're already . . ."

The mere possibility of not being able to calm his
nerves made the shivers worse. His breath rattled
through his teeth, asthmatic. "Been sitting fishing," he
gasped. "Too cold . . . pneumonia, maybe, if I
can't . . . the doctor said spirits . . ."

Then the kid couldn't let him have the rum fast
enough, tried to call a doctor, the works. But he got
away.

The girl on the beach never wore anything but canvas
shoes, jeans, and a sweater three times too large.
Sometimes her long black hair blew loose in the wind,

sometimes she wore it in a single prim braid that hung almost to her waist.

When she wasn't there, the long stretch of sand was empty. Desolate. He would watch the tenth floor windows and wait. He angled his chair so that he could keep his eye on her building while he fished. He wanted to know if anything had happened with the young officer. He was willing to lay bets . . .

"I was afraid you were sick," she said, and he almost fell off his chair.

"Jesus!" he spluttered, lurching round and clutching at his heart. "Don't *do* that!"

"Sorry. Didn't mean to scare you." She had a deep voice, almost gravelly, but soft, full of smoke and mist. "When you weren't on the beach yesterday . . . Have you been all right?"

Embarrassing, the way it pleased him that she had noticed his absence. "Jussa . . . ju . . . just a touch of old age," he stammered, but it came out self-pitying instead of sardonic as he'd intended. The way she stared at him, gravely, right between the eyes! It made him flounder. Once upon a time, girls lowered their gaze; you saw their lashes and the blush on their cheeks. Good girls, that is. If they didn't do this, you knew something right there.

"Are you all right now?" she persisted.

"Fit to fish all night." But his voice was playing up, sliding and slipping about, turning scratchy, as though he were nothing more than a show-off in a schoolyard.

She said earnestly, "You can sit still for so long in the cold, it's amazing. I wish I could learn your secret."

He laughed, a crude sharp sound, startled. "My secret?"

"Your patience. Your tranquillity."

He had to laugh again, it was involuntary. Him, the

original cantankerous, irritable husband, father, grandfather. In Mosman and Cremorne, his daughters braced
themselves for his visits. He didn't know what to say.
He gestured vaguely at the surf, tongue-tied.

"Yes," she said. "I know. That's why I come here
too. On Saturday, there were skindivers in around the
rocks up there." She pointed to the Long Reef end of
the beach. "That would be even better, I think. I wish I
were a stronger swimmer."

"You'd freeze —" But he checked himself from telling her she'd freeze her tits off. "You'd turn yourself
blue," he said.

"They had wetsuits on."

"Just the same." He couldn't fit her into a past or
present. She was as different from the bottle shop girl
with green-streaked hair as a star is from tinsel. He
couldn't think of anyone less like his teenage grand-
daughters. She was not of course the kind of granddaughter he would deserve. More the kind Lew might
have had if he hadn't stayed on in New Guinea.
"Anyhow, you'd take such an awful battering on the
rocks."

"I don't know." Her smile was strange, secret, full of
private desire. "I think it would be nice. One of the
divers told me that if you stay down deep . . . below the
surf, you know . . . there are caves down there. He said
it was still as a church. He said there were fish that glowed like lamps." She drew something in the wet sand with
a pointed toe; it might have been a flame, or perhaps
just a crooked line. "It's only when you have to come
up through the surf . . . He had blood all over his face
and hands from the reef, but he dived back in." She
gazed down the beach at the rocks, smiling her dreamy
smile. "I would like to see those caves."

In the time she might have come from, he thought,

she was the kind who would have worn a hairshirt and whipped herself with penitential cat-o'-nine-tails. He understood why nuns drove soldiers to rape; and old men to dreams.

Old men, old men. He was where he belonged: in one of the rooming houses strung along the Pittwater Road, a club of sorts. The rooming houses were desiccated outside and in by the corrosions of sea salt and of stubborn cardiovascular systems that went on pumping breath and even hope through an assortment of derelicts, all of them left stranded by old age and widowerhood. He picked his way along the high tide line. He knew this route, messy, wavering, a shifting seaweedy border.

Nothing was stable.

Housemates came and went, anything could claim them: death, a son or daughter whose conscience got the upper hand for a while, loss of memory. (Sometimes the police returned a dazed lodger from the ferry docks at Manly, or from Wynyard Station.)

Cockroaches whispered to one another when Gabe came in, snickering among their dustballs. He crumpled up another newspaper (someone's find at the pub) and stuffed it into the window space. Perhaps he should learn skindiving. Stranger things, he believed, had been accomplished by old men.

He took off his coat and laid it on the bed. He huddled under it.

Something glowed in the corner of a dream. It was the girl.

Once, when the tide was fully in, he saw her standing on the rocks at the end of the beach and thought she was going to dive in. The shivers hit him.

She's a loony, he thought. A real loony.

There was absolutely nothing he could do. It would take him at least ten minutes to reach her.

If he saved her, would it cancel out the other?

She just stood there, a silhouette against the sky and the waves, while the morning did a slow hapless slide towards noon, and ten thousand cars made their zombie way along the Pittwater Road to Manly and the Harbour Bridge. The spray threw itself around her in a frenzy, she must have been drenched.

He watched, shivering, until miraculously she turned and picked her way back across the rocks, leggy as a gull.

He was trembling with anxiety and outrage. Long before she reached him, he could smell — or fancied he could smell — her body heat, her denims steaming at the crotch, the musty soaked wool of her sweater. He left his fishing rod propped against his chair and hobbled to meet her like a broken toy, overwound. He planned to take her by the shoulders and shake her. You'll catch your death, he planned to shout.

He was stopped short, however, by her radiance.

There was no other word for it.

She brushed the sodden tendrils of hair out of her eyes and asked, puzzled, "Is something the matter?"

Now the army ducks came rumbling nightly, two by two, through sleep. They were crowded with the past, packed tight with faces pale as communion wafers. Lew's face was always among them, his eyes on Gabe no matter how Gabe twisted and turned.

Once, Gabe staggered out of bed and shouted: "Damn it, won't you ever let up?"

Someone else with a hangover came reeling in and offered a tumbler of booze and an oath.

In the morning, the shivers came, a daily companion.

Gabe dosed himself with rum chasers, he headed for the beach with his fishing gear, he waited for the girl.

He had decided she could save him.

He had decided she was a visitant from somewhere outside of the known. He had only to look at the girls who hung around the newsagent's or the fish and chip shop, snapping gum, sucking on cigarettes, dressed in cheap tight clothes, to know that he was right. She belonged in a different dimension.

He would watch her paddle her way along that shimmering nowhere, that space between sand and sea where the undertow fans its fluted way back to the deep, her canvas shoes laced together and slung over her shoulders like the nubs of clipped wings. Her oversized sweater was infinitely suggestive. It was pure as a nun's habit.

That kind of person, he thought (and he meant, vaguely, white witches, crazies, saints) that kind of person has a certain *touch*, a gift. If he could walk into the circle of light that came from her . . . It was a kind of underwater luminousness, the sort that tropical fish gave off in deep caves.

He became obsessed.

He watched the tenth floor of the concrete building, he became an expert on the movement of curtains, the language of lights switched on and off, of shades raised. He watched by day, and also by night when the sand crackled with frost and the skin of his fingers swelled and split from the cold. He plotted her routes.

One night, as he shivered down by the water's edge, he was certain he saw her standing naked at the tenth floor window. He considered seriously, then, the question of whether he had become nothing more than a dirty old man.

But he absolved himself.

It was something else altogether.

She was on to him though. That kind of person knows when her powers are being sapped, and it got harder and harder to cross her path. He would see the cream-coloured fisherman's sweater, like a peace flag, against the cliff or the rocks. He would wait and wait. And then finally a fluttering up at the tenth floor would catch his eye, a window opening or closing. She had given him the slip again. Yet if he walked along the Pittwater Road to the top of the cliff, she would take the beach route.

In dreams, on the bad nights, Gabe would wave the girl's sweater. *Truce, truce!* he would plead, and the magic worked. Lew would smile. He would give the thumbs up sign. I'm OK, he would call. Save your own skin, for god's sake; that's what you're *supposed* to do.

There was a bad spell when he did not so much as catch a glimpse of the girl for three days. The beach was grey. Fish avoided his line. His pension cheque was late — the threatened postal strike? — and he had to take a bus into the city to see about it. The bus was much too full of rude teenagers who might have belonged to a different race altogether from the girl. No one gave him a seat. It rained.

He waited in line to see about his cheque. You should have got it, they told him; it has already gone out in the mail. If you haven't received it by Friday, come and see us again. No one offered him an advance for the purpose of buying a beer in the pub near Wynyard Station. He thought of calling his Mosman daughter, or the one in Cremorne, but decided not to. Instead he waited in line for the return bus, which was late. At the Spit Bridge it was stalled in traffic for an hour. When he finally got off in front of the Collaroy Post Office, he walked along the length of the beach without any hope and stood on the rocks. There was no sign of the girl. The rain was not heavy, merely spiteful and persistent, and he was soaked to the skin. He could feel the cold everywhere. It was a dark time.

He did not expect the shivers or the weather to lift again.

"Have you been fishing all night?" she asked, startling him.

Her dark hair was fanned loose over her shoulders, she paddled into the shallows in front of his chair, the morning sun was behind her. He squinted into the light, his eyes watering.

"Where have you been?" he demanded.

"Oh, I had to . . . you know. I come and go. But you're *always* here, you're as reliable as morning. Do you fish all night?"

He shook his head, not trusting himself to speak. He could feel July squirming like an eel, making way for August, could feel the warmth coming back. In front of him was nothing but brightness, so much sun on the water. He could barely see.

"Have you caught anything?" she asked.

"Oh yes," he laughed.

"What?"

"What's your name?"

"Look!" she said. "The army ducks are coming back. Training exercises. They do it every few weeks, he told me. He said they'd be here again today."

"So you saw him again," he accused.

"Who?"

"The young officer." (Really, this was ridiculous, this grief, this jealousy.) "I thought I saw him paying court."

"Paying court!" She repeated the words as though they were objects in glass cases, fragile beyond belief, evoking wonder and amusement. *"Paying court!"* She laughed and flung up her arms and did an odd pirouette in the water. "You remind me of my grandfather. You make me wish . . ."

"What?" he prompted.

"Oh, you know. For some time before all the mistakes."

"Mistakes," he sighed. What would she know about mistakes? The army ducks were close enough now that he could see the little yellow oilskinned blobs, toy men on obsolete make-believe boats.

"Would you believe," he said, "in New Guinea at the end of the war, I watched them drive hundreds of those things into the sea and scuttle them? Hundreds of them."

"They sank them? But why?"

"Blessed if I know. Not that any of us cared. The war was over and they'd flown in beer and we cheered when each bloody duck went under."

The girl stared at the approaching ships. "The man my grandmother was engaged to was killed in New Guinea. That was before my grandfather, of course, but I guess she never really got over it. She used to talk about him sometimes, I suppose she felt I was safe. She always kept his AIF badge in her underwear drawer. Hey, are you okay?"

"It's nothing. These shivers come and go."

"Doesn't *look* like nothing. You want me to help you back to your house?"

"No, no. Your young officer is coming." He could make sacrifices, he was not incapable of nobility.

"Oh, *my young officer*." She laughed, a haunting sound. He thought of novices in a cloister listening to a nearby circus, seeing only skyrockets and the tip of the ferris wheel. But she is more remote from men than that, he thought; she puts up a higher wall. The energy, the light that she gave off — he sensed it came from stamping out the constant fires that flared from stray sparks.

"My young officer," she said again. "You mean the one with the offbeat tastes? So you think you can pick my type, do you?"

"Your type?" He never knew what to expect from her. "I didn't think you had a . . ."

"Yes," she said lightly. "The wrong type. Come on, let me take you home."

He thought if she touched him, he would catch fire. He would go up in smoke, a blissful death. But the moment had to be right — not with temptation leaping onto the beach from an army duck, distracting her.

"I'm all right," he said. "It's nothing. I'm better off sitting out here in the sun. The last three days were terrible."

"Oh well. Winter. We can't complain." But she looked oddly disconsolate, as though reminded of something unpleasant. She dropped unexpectedly onto the sand beside him and began scooping out channels with her hands. The creeping wavelets filled them, they silted up, she scooped out fresh canals. "Oh well," she said again, as though lengthy deliberations had been concluded. "So. New Guinea. Did you lose many mates?"

He was caught off guard. "Lew," he blurted, and stopped. The long slow loss, so unlike Lew who did everything else like a bull in a china shop. He wanted to tell her: "It took hours, and there wasn't a thing I could . . . Snipers thick as flies, it would have been useless.

"Nevertheless, nevertheless . . .

"There were men who did that kind of thing. There are widows who keep the Victoria Cross, awarded posthumously, in their underwear drawers . . .

"Once I heard him call my name and I couldn't move for terror and nausea. Lew himself was the kind who would have rushed straight out and thought later . . ."

He said none of this. He said only: "Everyone lost mates. It was a bad time."

She looked at him out of her grave unwavering eyes. "Your generation," she said, "you give something off, you know? A kind of strength, or . . . I don't know, you're *real*, that's what it is. It's because you've *done* things with your lives."

Oh Jesus, he couldn't stand it, a fraud like him. "Listen," he began. He had to confess.

"Just seeing you sitting here every day," she said, "a part of the beach . . ."

Oh Jesus. This had to be the moment. Now he had to confess and now she had to touch him.

The first army duck was waddling into the shallows, ungainly, its webbed wheels feeling for sand. It lurched out of the muffling water and the roar of its engine spattered them.

She put her hands over her ears and said urgently: "Let's get away from here. Let's go down to the rocks." He could barely hear her over the engines and the even louder thudding of his jubilant heart. She paused: "Oh, but your chair. And your fishing rod."

He cared not a pin for them. He dismissed them with a wave of his hand. From the army duck, the young officer was scanning the beach. Too late, too late, Gabe telegraphed; you lost. When the girl took his arm he could feel himself dissolving into light. By the time they reached the rocks, he was weightless, nothing but pared-down soul. Far away, the trio of army ducks wheeled in meaningless circles, spitting sand. On either side of the girl and himself, the surf seethed into chasms and leaped skyward, anointing them with spray. The girl was rapt, she appeared to him translucent, there was a light inside her.

"I have to keep coming here," she said. "I have to."

"I know." He understood. He understood she was not what she seemed. "I know what you really are."

She raised her eyebrows, startled, and looked at him: a shocked look that hung there and then dwindled into sadness. Then she got up and picked her delicate way across the rocks to the last tall peak above the caves. She stood poised there, but he felt neither apprehension nor time passing.

She turned at last and came back and sat beside him in the niche near the cliff.

"So even here it shows," she said heavily. "I suppose that's inevitable."

"Yes," he said. "It is, I think." He'd known, really, from the moment she had mentioned the seminary tower at Manly.

"Anyway," she said, "today's my last day, what's the use? I'm going back."

"Would you still let . . .? I'd like to see you from time to time, if you wouldn't mind."

Her eyes widened. He counted thirty seconds by the thump of his heart. "Even you?" she said at last.

"It's forbidden?"

"Oh," she shrugged. "Nothing's forbidden."

"Well then," he said. "When would be a suitable time?"

It seemed to him that the air itself was bruising the skin around her eyes. She is seeing my death, he thought. He put out his hand to touch her arm and she flinched. There were tears — or it could have been salt spray — in her lashes.

"Don't be sad," he said. "I really don't mind."

The army ducks were wheeling back into the sea. He watched them as in a dream. They seemed impossibly distant, matchbox toys, quaint mementoes of a time long gone.

"No, I suppose not," the girl said. "Come whenever you want, why not?"

She stood up and shaded her eyes as the ships sailed towards North Head and the Sydney Harbour docks. They were smaller, swan-like, graceful again. She brushed her cheeks with the back of one hand and tossed back her hair and began to sing in a sweet reedy voice:

I saw three ships come sailing in,
On Christmas Day, on Christmas Day . . .

Still singing, she turned and stepped in her gull-like way across the rocks towards the cliff. "Wait!" he called, stumbling after and almost pitching himself into surf. "How will I find you?"

"Just ask at the Cross," she called back.

Which one, which one? Holy Cross? The convent in Dee Why? She was getting further away. He felt panicky, desolate, he slipped again and gashed his arm. He had to stop. He didn't even know her name.

"I don't know your name," he shouted.

She was climbing the cliff face now. "Just ask for Angela," she called. "I'm well known. Fantasies a specialty."

"What?" he shouted. "I can't hear you."

She kept on climbing.

He leaned against a rock and watched till she disappeared over the top of the cliff. She did not look back. That was the way it was with visitations. You couldn't hang on to them. But he thought he caught pieces of her singing drifting back in the wind:

And who do you think was in those ships,
On Christmas Day, on Christmas Day?
'Twas Jesus Christ and His La-die
On Chris . . .

Bondi

At twenty-six, Leigh (who is Cass's cousin) is tired of playing the part of bad girl but the habit is difficult to break. She fell into the role quite naturally at puberty — parsons' daughters do — and played it to the hilt, and now it's like a skin she can't shed. The thing is, Cass decides, Leigh knows the ropes of badgirl land, and even though the terrain has become tedious (has in fact become as boring as the Sunday afternoon prayer meetings of their childhoods), Leigh feels comfortable there. And safe.

Safe? In a manner of speaking, safe; because Cass, watching Leigh smooth suntan oil on her bare breasts, knows that Leigh wouldn't even count the Hanlon affair. Leigh wouldn't give it any more significance than Cass would give a crunched fender or a smashed-up headlight. Annoying, yes. Inconvenient. But (shrug) these things happen, and besides, every life needs a little excitement, right?

Nevertheless, it is because of Hanlon that Leigh has called, and because of Hanlon that they are lying towel by towel on Bondi beach, with Deb making sandcastles a few yards off. Not the usual way for Cass to spend a Saturday afternoon these days.

"Come on, Cass," Leigh had said. "Live a little."

"Well . . ." Cass hears herself again, all tiresome caution. She is torn between maternal anxiety and the pleasant pinpricks of risk. *(Live* a little? Being target practice for Hanlon?) "There's this finger-painting thingamy at the public library. I was going to take Deb . . ."

Leigh already has the stroller out. "Deb needs to be *out*doors, not in. What kind of an Aussie kid are you raising here?"

"But will it be safe?"

"Safe as Sunday School. Hanlon's so dumb, he'll still be watching my flat in Melbourne."

Leigh and Cass have travelled different roads, but they need each other. We're heads and tails, I suppose you could say, Cass explains to Tom. Though Leigh always counters: *You're* the wolf in sheep's clothing, and I'm the little lost lamb playing wolf to protect myself. (Black and white, Tom hopes; night and day.) At any rate, each plays Best Supporting Actress to the other's role. They grew up in Brisbane, which should explain a lot, and were fed milk and biblical verses in their highchairs.

When Leigh telephoned, the day before yesterday, Cass could feel the rush at the top of her head. "Leigh!" She was laughing already. "I don't believe it, I thought you'd vanished from the face of the land! Where are you? Brisbane?"

"God no! Not Brizzy." Leigh hasn't been heard from for two years, though the family gossip mill has been murmuring Townsville, Cairns, Kuranda, Daintree, Leigh heading further and further north, heading deeper into shady reasons, bad company, offshore boats, *Darwin!* (in a shocked whisper), Cape Trib, Thursday Island *(grant her Thy mercy, Lord)*, New Guinea! Then Brisbane again, it was rumoured. Someone had seen her at Expo, her hair un-gelled and unspiked, looking like a normal person, and she'd said *In sales,* giving a phone number. (Selling . . .? No one dared to ask what.) At the phone number, a male voice went off in a shower of expletives and detonations about that fucking bitch who'd moved on, bloody lucky for her, and if he ever fucking caught up with the slut . . .

Lost traces, lost causes, lost sheep. The family sighed and bowed its head: *Remember, O Lord, thy wayward child and turn not Thy face away from* . . .

"I'm here," Leigh says. "In Sydney." Excitement, salamander style, comes slinking in through Cass's eardrum and makes straight for all her nerve centres of temptation. "Listen," Leigh says. "I need a place to crash, it's sort of urgent."

Cass picks her up at Circular Quay. "God, you look —" *terrible,* but what does it matter? Reinstated as bailer-out-in-chief, Cass feels giddy with pleasure.

"Yeah, well. I've been doing a bit of coke. Doesn't go very well with food." Leigh lights a cigarette. "How's Deb?"

"Adorable. You'll see in a minute. Tom's home, so I just rushed out."

"And have you been a good girl while I've been gone?" Leigh asks.

They both laugh.

"What happened?" Cass wants to know.

"What do you mean?"

"You said it was urgent."

"Oh, that." Leigh shrugs. "Nothing much. You remember Hanlon?"

"That bloke you were living with in Brisbane?"

"Him. We hit the road for a while, business you know, but I got tired of doing the dirty work and taking shit, so I —"

"What sort of shit?"

"Oh, you know, the usual. He hit me round a bit."

"Leigh, why? *Why* do you keep latching on to men like that? You've gotta stop —"

"Yeah, I know. I've tried, I really have. I just can't seem to get turned on unless they're hellraisers. Anyway, in Brizzy, Hanlon set up this little dream of a deal, with me in the hot seat, natch, and it came to me that I could just take the money and run. So I did. Ripped him off for twenty thousand, and headed for Melbourne."

"God, Leigh! Twenty thousand dollars!" Cass is appalled, her eyes glitter, she is full of plans. "Well . . ." — she can't stop reeling from the enormity of it — "Well, now you can afford to, you know, quit . . . Quit, uh, selling. You can go straight, get an apartment here, finish your degree . . . "

"Never give up, do you?" Leigh says fondly. In high school, they had been neck and neck. Leigh had won a state medal as well as a Commonwealth Scholarship. A brilliant future, her teachers said, which turned out to be true in a way. "Still," Leigh sighs. "Mackie was worth it for a while." She winces, then smiles, then winces again, remembering Mackie, the ex-con she'd run off with before the end of her first year at Queensland Uni. "About going back . . . I think about it a lot, but I dunno after all these years."

"It's never too late."

"Yeah, yeah." Leigh is wistful. "I meant to, actually. Use the money for, you know, uni or something. But I blew it all on coke in Melbourne and last week I saw —"

"You blew *twenty thousand dollars?*"

"Well, not just me. Friends, you know. I threw a few parties. And I guess the word got round because last week —"

"It's all gone?" Cass is awestruck. "That *entire* amount?"

"'Fraid so." Leigh twists sideways in the seat, leaning against the passenger door, to gauge the effect of her words on Cass. "My coke's at maintenance level, though. It's under control."

"I get frightened for you," Cass says. (If Leigh weren't around, what would happen to the world on its axis? What might Cass have to do?)

"Yeah, me too sometimes." Leigh laughs. "Anyway, last week I saw Hanlon watching my place. He doesn't take kindly to being gypped, so I thought I'd better bugger off. Hitch-hiked up, left early yesterday and just arrived. God, I'm tired."

She slept for fifteen hours. She woke, she ate something, she threw up, she slept, she sleeps.

Tom, looking into the guest room before heading for his office (the Saturday catch-up), says: "God, it's the worst I've ever seen her. She's thin as a whippet." Except for her tits, he thinks. In spite of himself, he's stirred. The unspiked black hair, longer now, shaggy and glossy, falls across a child's face. He kisses Cass brusquely: "So how long is she planning to camp here?" Not that he's made uneasy by Leigh's presence in his house, not really. Because this is what Tom has observed: that the children of True Believers go one of two ways, and that there is a delicate ecology within families. To Tom's legal mind (he's a partner in a Regent Street law firm), Leigh is some sort of warranty.

Leigh wakes into high sun. "Let's go to the beach," she says.

"Well . . . There's this finger-painting thing-amy . . ."

"Live a little," Leigh laughs, exasperated.

And so they push the stroller along the neat residential streets of Bellevue Hill and down the long asphalt slope to Bondi. Cass is always mildly surprised that no one asks for her passport at that point where the buildings change so sharply.

Cass watches the way the men walk up and down where the sand turns hard, the way their equipment strains against their skimpy briefs, the way their eyes, not even pretending to be covert, scan the rows of oil-slicked breasts: the peacock parade on its mating route between towels and bodies. It still surprises Cass, the lack of self-consciousness on all sides. Bare bosoms are so common that if she rolls sideways on her towel and squints, the beach appears to be strewn with egg cartons, pointy little mounds in all directions. Big ones and small ones, floppy ones and tight little cones. She considers: if I took off my top, would Deb be startled? Would Leigh? (And if *Tom* heard of it?) A man walks within eight inches of her head, flicking sand in her eyes, and manages to spill beer on Leigh's midriff. Leigh sits bolt upright and her splendid bare breasts bounce and quiver.

"Jeez, sorry." The man squats down, blotting at beer-wet skin with his towel.

"Oh, bugger off," Leigh says without malice.

"Hey, an accident, swear to God!" The man turns toward Cass and winks. He has very white teeth and a dimple beside his chin. Cass has an urge to stick out her tongue, throw sand at him maybe, and a simultaneous one to run her fingers down through the hair on his chest, across the flat tanned belly, across the blue lycra welt to that bleat of skin on the inside of his squatting thighs. Baby skin, and she can't take her eyes off it. She'd forgotten this: the way sun and salt air and drowsiness and the smell of suntan oil add up to lust.

Not lust exactly. More a sort of catholic sensuousness, an erotic languor toward the whole wide world.

"Got some beer in the Esky," the man says. "Wanna join me?"

"Sure," Cass murmurs silkily, eyes meeting his. "Why not?"

"Be right back."

Cass stretches like a cat and reaches behind and unhooks her bikini top. She squirts a glob of sunscreen into one palm and rubs it lovingly on her nipples.

"What the hell are you doing?" Leigh asks. "Why'd you invite that jerk back here? We'll never get rid of him."

Cass smiles. This feels good, very good: sun on her white and private breasts, it's like losing your virginity again, a lifesaver watching while she massages in the oil, a slow rhythmic caress, auto-erotic. Watching herself being watched, she can feel what it was that hooked Narcissus.

"A married woman!" Leigh is agitated, Leigh is suddenly and inexplicably angry. "A *mother!* Put your clothes back on, we're going."

Cass's eyes go wide. "You've got to be kidding."

"You think you're funny or something? You think you're —"

Then chaos comes in a skirl of sand. First, the Esky man is knocked for a sixer, the blue Esky sails in an arc toward the surf trailing cans of Swan Lager like so many bows on a kite tail. After that, it's helter-skelter: screaming, cursing, an assortment of missiles (footballs, cricket bats, a rubber skipping-rope), bodies lunging, bodies falling, blood. There are gouts of blood on the sand. Mothers scream and gather up tots and towels, heading for the concrete steps. Cass scoops up Deb and runs to the water. Children cry and don't know if they're crying from fear or from the sand in their eyes. People wipe their wet faces and find themselves sprinkled with blood. A little further off, a ring of boys gathers to watch and barrack. This is some fight, some thrill.

It's wogs! The wogs started it. They were bothering a white girl, they threw sand in a white lady's face, they kicked a football right into a little kid's head, a little white kid, he's got concussion. Theories fly as fast as punches, as thick as blood. *Go get 'em, send the buggers back where they bloody came from.*

On the concrete embankment that separates beach from shore road, the gasping out-of-condition mothers watch with bemusement, the way one watches a battle scene in a movie. Here and there a ghastly detail catches the eye, but no one can tell who is fighting whom, or who is winning, though it's broken beer bottle time now, it's getting ugly. Time to blow the whistle.

And so the lifesavers come in their tanned and bleach-blond ranks, barefoot, high-cut bikinis exposing their golden buttocks, skullcaps in place, oars from the lifeboats flailing at air and insurrection. It's the jousts: there are pennants (the Bondi club pennant, and also — how did they come to be in the mix? — the pennants of the Dee Why and Curl Curl clubs); there are broken lances, broken oars, there are gasping damsels in a swoon of distress, wearing nothing more than a scrap of fabric between the legs. The venerable order of the Knights Templar of the Bondi Surf Lifesaving Club, aided by the Knights Templar of Dee Why, Curl Curl, and Collaroy, runs on the double and tilts at the windmill of Crusade.

Sirens now! It's a full scale rout, it's epic, it's newspaper and television stuff, there are squad cars, an ambulance, an ABC cameraman. (How did the news travel so fast?) And here are the police, truncheons raised, all blue-serge efficiency and ocker sentiment, here are the upholders of the Australian way of decency, *howya goin' mate? it's a free country, we don't mind wogs on the beach if they behave themselves but if they're gonna muck the place up, well they're bloody not gonna know what hit them, are they?* Ah, here are the police running on the double in their shiny black lace-up shoes, here are the police floundering through soft sucking sand, here are the Keystone Cops.

The wogs are fleeing. Born into Palestinian camps, winners of immigration and fitness lotteries, full of street smarts and survival instincts, the wogs are very very fleet of foot. There's a long line haring south toward Cronulla, single file: the wogs (there are only ten of them actually, mostly teenagers, Palestinian kids, a few in their twenties perhaps), then the swift lifesavers (about thirty of these), then the ragtag posse of original combatants (the local Bondi and Darlinghurst boys, beer-bellied, a little flabby, falling back), then the dozen sand-wallowing cops, then the cameraman.

Young boys hop and dance on the sand in a frenzy of excitement, little bookies in the making, calling bets. The line is thinning out now, it's single file with bigger and bigger spaces between the dots. It's going to be a clean getaway, no one's laying odds, the tension's gone. Towels and blankets and buckets and spades and bodies move into the vacuum. Someone turns a radio on. The sand settles quickly.

Where's Leigh? Cass, disconsolate and shaken, spreads her towel and looks about for the stroller and Deb's bucket and spade. Deb, paddling down in the water all this bloody while, is unaffected, and talks confidentially to the shells in her pink hands. Cass sees the stroller, which has travelled thirty feet or so and is almost undamaged.

One by one, the heroes — the local boys — return. *Good on yer, mate!* They swagger a little and flaunt their battle scars: the bloodied mouths, busted teeth, purple welts. It turns out to have been an argument about a frisbee, a Palestinian frisbee which had sailed right across a true blue volleyball game without benefit of visa or *may I please?* Directly in the frisbee's path had been the head of a local boy. *Bloody wogs come out here and think they own the bloody beach.* Little clusters of veterans, hobbling, grumbling, strutting, climb the concrete stairs and cross the street to the Bondi Beach Hotel.

Deb struggles valiantly up from the shallows with a bucket of water and empties it at Cass's feet. Avidly, she watches the sand suck at her offering, watches the wet funnel form. "Where does it go, Mummy?"

"It goes to China." A boy says this, a passing teenage boy who, as it turns out, is in urgent need of a listener. He is full of important information which pushes against the aching skin of his body, a body in which he is not at ease. He flops down and arranges all his arms and legs beside the child.

"You got a big bitey," Deb tells him solemnly, running her small pink and wondering finger across his cheek. A purple welt, like a brand from a poker, makes a diagonal from mouth to ear.

"Yeah," he says, speaking to the child but needing her mother's reaction. "I'm the one that got hit with the frisbee." He waits. He hasn't quite decided whether to be victim or hero, he needs an audience, a sounding-board. "I'm the one got the whole thing started." Cass can see on the surface of his skin — the pulsing tics, the flinches — a *pas de deux* of swagger and self-pity. While his hands offer their services to Deb (packing the wet sand for her, tamping it into her bucket, tapping it neatly out into pristine castle) his toes clasp and unclasp sand. Beneath the backwash of battle, he is locating a surf of emotions. "And then me mates bugger off to the pub and leave me." The wound of his under-age status hurts like hell; he feels the purple scar gingerly, and Cass can see him translating, interpreting, deciding: he's victim, definitely victim, abandoned, cruelly neglected. His head is throbbing. "It's me Saturday off," he says forlornly. "Gotta work shift again tomorrow. It's me only day for the beach."

Cass touches his cheek. "You should get that cut attended to."

"Me dad's gonna give me hell, the police and all." His voice breaks. "You notice how they only go in gangs?" he asks bitterly, blinking hard, turning away. "Those bloody cowards, bloody wogs." He jumps up and runs into the surf.

Cass gathers up towels and Deb, and drags the stroller through sand. No sign of Leigh. The walk home is twice as long as the walk to the beach.

Leigh is in the enclosed back patio, sitting in Tom's favourite deckchair and drinking beer with a guest, a young man in his twenties, olive-skinned, very striking. A clump of the visitor's abundant black hair is matted with blood, and there is a dried crosshatching of blood around his right eye and right cheek. Cass remembers the moment when a cricket bat hit that temple with a sick *thook* of sound.

"Oh Cass!" Leigh calls gaily. "This is Mahmoud Khan."

Cass feels shy and ungainly in her own backyard.

"How d'you do?" she says awkwardly, extending her hand.

Courtly, Mahmoud Khan takes it and kisses the backs of her fingers. He smiles with his dazzling white teeth.

"I felt it was the least I could do," Leigh explains.

Cass, confused, is remembering the single file running toward Cronulla and cannot figure out how Leigh, how this young man . . .

Leigh says: "I hailed a taxi and followed, and when they ducked up to the road and across and into the alley behind the Khan restaurant . . ." She shrugs.

"They never catch us," Mahmoud says, and his accent is broad Australian, more or less, with unpredictable slides and riffs. He smiles his dazzling smile. "We know Bondi like we know a woman's body, all the ins and outs, we got signals, the buggers can't keep us off the beach. Free bloody country, right?" With the pads of his fingers, he explores the crusted lump on his temple. "We gotta go in teams, though, for protection."

Cass fumbles for words: "I'm awfully sorry . . . I'd, uh, like to apologise . . ."

Mahmoud Khan bows slightly, with only a hint of sarcasm, and Cass feels like a gauche schoolgirl who has just said something particularly banal. She blunders on nevertheless: "We're not all like that." Mahmoud Khan bows again and his movement seems to take in the wisteria arbour, the graceful white enamelled chairs, the expensive interlocked paving.

"Well," Leigh says, jumping up. "We'll be off." Moving in front of Mahmoud, so that only Cass can see her, she raises her eyebrows significantly and smiles a little. "Mahmoud's family runs The Khan's Kitchen. We're going to have dinner there." She bends over to kiss Deb, gives Cass a hug. "I'll phone," she says.

* * *

On Sunday morning, Cass wakes at dawn and feels the absence of Leigh in the air. Tom is snoring softly. Is this contentment? Cass wonders dully, studying a long hairline crack in the ceiling. Is this peace? Against the crack, an image interposes itself: Mahmoud Khan is eating Leigh's buttered body. Cass cannot put a name to her feeling. She eases herself out of bed and pads barefoot into Deb's room. In the crib, her daughter's pale ringlets lie damp on the pillow and she bends over to smell the sweet-sour innocent morning breath — which is not entirely regular; which leaves Deb's parted lips in little syncopated riffs. Quick! Cass's hand flies to her own mouth to muffle a sound, an improper noise, some little peep of the body, a lurch of fear or loss, a sob perhaps. She is almost afraid to brush her lips against her daughter's cheek.

Sunday morning ticks by and she simply stands there, watching, trying to imagine the unimaginable: Deb at ten, fifteen, twenty. Then she tiptoes from the room, pulls on jeans and t-shirt and sandshoes, and lets herself out the front door. Not certain why she feels furtive, *illicit* even, she nevertheless treads softly as a cat past the neat accusing houses, down the long hill, across the desolate patio of the hotel, to the deserted beach. She takes off her sandshoes and ties them together and slings them round her neck. She could be the only person, the loneliest person, in the world. Why? she asks the gregarious gulls. What do I want? She does not know the answer to either question. She walks, giving her heels and toes a little twist at each step for the pleasure of it.

Ouch! Stumbling, clutching at her right foot, she sees the hypodermic she has stepped on. She stares at it in a dazed uncomprehending way, knowing it has a meaning she must grope for. She thinks vaguely of Leigh and

Mahmoud Khan and her daughter's cheek damp on its pillow. Then she notices another hypodermic, just ten inches away. Then another. And something else: condoms, she realises. She starts to count them, ten, twenty, thirty, more, just from where she is standing. She shades her eyes and looks about her. There are hundreds of condoms and hypodermics. In a high strange breathy voice, she recites aloud to the gulls: *And she sees the vision splendid / Of the sunlit sands extended* . . . Nervous laughter breaks through her lips like bubbles.

This is the spot, she thinks, where Deb was playing with her bucket and spade.

In the distance, she can see the sandsweeper beginning its daily work, the tractor ploughing through sand, the mesh drum gulping in dreck and leaving a plume of pure sifted gold in its wake. She watches it, mesmerised. She knows what she wants now. She wants to go back one half hour in time, to be brushing her lips against Deb's unblemished cheek. She wants to go back two whole days, to the moment when she picked up Leigh at Circular Quay. She wants to go back a decade, a decade and a half, to the day when she and Leigh sat high in the mango tree and showed each other their first underarm hairs. Her foot hurts. She watches the sandsweeper, unable to move.

Over the roar of his engine, the sandsweeper shouts and waves. She cannot catch his words. She is thinking of something she has read about turtles: how thousands of them hatch high up on the beach and begin their mad race for the water; and how the gulls scream and dive; and how only the merest fraction of the baby turtles reaches the waves.

The Chameleon Condition

Adam first became aware of his condition one midnight, or thereabouts, in his lover's bedroom. It seemed a trick of the moonlight. Yes, he was awed, of course he was, he never ceased to be awed by the translucent quality of her skin — but it was not that. He was lying on his back and she was kneeling astride him, her breasts and her spicy perfume filling the sensory foreground. Her long hair flung itself about everywhichway in the wind of her gallop.

And there beyond her agile limbs lay his own legs, foreshortened from his pillow's-eye perspective, parted slightly, itching (it was *like* an itch) with pleasure, and . . .

And . . .?

Startled, he raised his head slightly from the pillow. His legs were bright blue with gratification. Blue as a peacock's feather. Blue as Krishna when the milkmaids licked him with their thousand tongues.

My god, look . . .! he would have cried out, except that a wave of sexual delirium barrelled into him at that very instant, his breath was knocked to kingdom come, he was caught and tossed overandover, he and his long-haired sea-horse racing neck and neck, a shoreline coming at them at a furious pace.

His lover (she was one of his colleagues at the university) flung back her hair and laughed. "I love it when you do that."

"Do what?"

"Grunt and moan and babble like a baby."

"Grumt?" he mumbled, embarrassed. *"Brabble?"* And she laughed again.

"My legs," he said, curious, incredulous, staring at them. It must have been the moon through the curtains. "Look at the way my legs are . . . But why isn't it happening to you?" His arms too, he saw them, confounded. And his belly, his chest. It was an incandescence, like marsh fire.

"Look," he said, a little frightened now, holding up his arm. But the light changed, or perhaps his endorphins calmed down, and the cobalt shrank away from his extremities, condensing, darkening, bolting toward the tiny opening in his shrivelled cock and disappearing as though he had sucked it back inside himself.

"God," he said shakily. He made an effort to laugh. "Did you see that?"

"What?" She opened a drowsy eye. She smiled. "You're so . . . ." Like a child in a toy shop, she might have said. She found it endearing, a man in his fifties so innocent, so touchingly inept.

"God!" he said. "Oh my god, the *time*." He groped for clothing, he kept a wary eye on his skin, he stumbled in the ropey noose of sheets. It made him jumpy the way she always kept him later than he intended, well not kept him perhaps, not exactly *kept* him. But she could hardly be said to be overly sensitive to the risks, to the situation, to the condition in which he found himself, to the intricacies —

The phone rang, and his body jerked like a rabbit's when pellet guns are about.

She reached languidly across her pillow and answered it. "Hello?" she said, and his breath stuck in his throat, waiting.

"It's your wife." She had her hand over the receiver, she cradled it between her breasts and sat up cross-legged and let her hair fall forward, watching him gravely from under it. "Hey," she murmured. "Hey, just kidding. If you could see yourself! You're white as a sheet."

And he was. Literally. He could barely see the pencil outline of his body against the bedding, white on white, a quick Picasso sketch.

"Hello?" his lover said into the receiver. "Hello?" She hung up. "Nobody there. Hey, are you all right?"

Was he all right? Maybe. Colour was returning to his flesh the way lilies sip up dyed water in florists' shops, in washed streaks. He stood, but felt queasy, and had to lean against her dresser while he pulled his trousers on.

"Actually, Adam," she said sombrely, quietly, biting her lip. "To tell you the truth, I think that *was* your wife. I get these calls, especially Friday and Saturday nights. The caller never speaks, but doesn't hang up either."

He leaned on her dresser and breathed slowly. He felt ill. If only his lover, or his wife, understood the intricacies.

His lover watched him carefully. "Except once," she said quietly. "About two weeks ago. The caller — it was a woman — asked me: 'Is Adam there?' Sounded very formal . . . like a secretary, say. But secretaries don't call in the middle of the night, do they?"

"Eve," he gasped. (Naturally his lover's name was Eve. She was, in fact, older than his wife though she seemed to him younger, he was not sure why. The career, he supposed. The vibrancy. His wife stayed home with the children and a sheen had gone from her, there was a certain listlessness . . .) "Eve, I can't . . ." He was having difficulty breathing. "I can't seem to . . ."

"You're hyperventilating. Here." She pulled the quilt over both of them, a cocoon. She let him sip carbon dioxide. "There." They surfaced into ordinary air. She said sympathetically: "You look awful. Do you need to . . .? C'mon." And she gave him her arm and helped him to the bathroom. "I shouldn't have said anything," she said remorsefully. "Of course, it could be anyone. It could be kids fooling around. It could have been a coincidence, a total fluke."

Adam kneeled in front of the toilet bowl, his turkey throat stretching, questing about, making strange sounds. He looked hideously comic, and Eve, distressed, had to turn away.

"Listen," she said. She filled the sink with warm water and soaked a facecloth in it. "Maybe I imagined she said Adam. The more I think about it, the more I convince myself I must have imagined it, because it's so unlikely, isn't it? No one actually *does* that sort of thing." She applied the wet facecloth to the back of his neck. "Does that feel better? You still look a bit green."

He managed to stand, then had to sit on the toilet seat, his head between his hands. He stared at his feet, seaweed-green, the colour spreading like wet mould.

"Listen." She stroked his hair, awkwardly tender. "I think it's better if you just stop coming, don't you?" He was so bourgeois, so cautious, so . . . well, tediously guilty, that it was like talking to a frightened child caught on the spikes of a new school.

He took deep breaths. He blinked several times, but the green did not go away. Indeed, if anything it seemed to be getting brighter, more nauseating; it was frog-green, swamp-green, the green of moss in old half-empty jam jars. "Can you see it?" he asked, terrified.

"I think we can both see it's the best thing," she said gently. "Not only for your own sake. And for hers, of course. But mine too. I mean, her silences . . . you've got to be awfully desperate . . . It's just not the sort of thing I do, Adam." She had learned to let happiness come and go, without anxiety. It always did keep coming again, in new and surprising shapes. "So I think it's better all round if you just stop —"

He clutched at her rather convulsively, and she had the awkward sensation of being his mother. "What can I do?" he sighed into the warm hollow between her breasts. "I feel so *desirous,* I feel ill with desire."

Eve was embarrassed. He had an oddly archaic vocabulary which she attributed to the afterglow of gilded academic prospects. Once he had been a golden boy, full of promise, but had slid downhill through a tunnel of marital mess and unrequited ambition into verbal pedantries, rejection slips from scholarly journals, and the big undergraduate classes. Still, he was an assiduous (his colleagues would have said "pushy") proposer of papers for overseas conferences, and a dogged reviewer and essayist for magazines edited by friends or by former students; and so he was warmed (though never quite sufficiently) by an inner vision of himself as under-appreciated Renaissance man. And as lover.

Sometimes he brought Beethoven's most mournful sonatas and played them endlessly and asked Eve: How like you this music, beloved?

Or: One of our colleagues opines, he would say of a certain new book.

Opines! Eve would think.

"Battersly opines . . ." he might say. "Though Frith

is of the opinion that . . ." He would mention other famous names he had met in overseas conference bars. (He had given the same lecture, under modified titles, in a number of countries.)

"And what do *you* opine?" she would ask, but he never seemed to hear the question.

Did Adam opine, ever? she wondered. Could he, all on his own, opine? Sometimes she found herself expecting him to give off the smell (distinctive, Edwardian, not unpleasant) of a second-hand bookstore. He made her feel ridiculously protective.

"I don't know what to do," he said on the night that his legs turned blue, then white, then green. He sucked her left breast, then her right. "My wife is given to many forms of subtle blackmail," he said mournfully. "But I can't give you up, Eve. I just can't. I couldn't live without you."

Eve patted him on the arm and handed him his shirt. There was a direct correlation, in her experience, between verbal extravagance and exits. *I am rash, I panic, I disappear.* The timidity of men was a source of wonder. The serpent, they said. The ripeness of the apple. The occasion. The woman tempted me. The wife forbids.

Was nobody ever at home?

Under all those belligerent layers, there was . . .?

"It's the children" he sighed. "My wife would threaten . . ."

"Adam," she said. He seemed to her lighter than air. "Let's just call it quits as fondly and sensibly as —"

"Some of our colleagues think you're playing sexual games with me," he complained fretfully.

"Do they? And what do you think?"

"I don't know what to think, I don't know what to . . . I think I'll take a . . . would a shower be all right, would you mind?"

For a moment she raised her eyebrows with surprise, but it was not an erotic invitation. Quite the contrary.

"Go ahead," she shrugged. (Odd how you could never quite prepare yourself for certain insults; how the glancing blow could cause unexpected pain.)

He scrubbed and scrubbed. He washed Eve's perfume from his pores. He showered until all the green had gone and the water ran clear and colourless down the drain.

It could have been his first wife who called, he thought as he drove home. His second wife never called him Adam, she had never cared to address him by a second-hand name, a *used* name, she had invented her own. So it could have been, must have been, his first wife. He did not for a moment doubt her malevolent powers, or her vigilance, in spite of all the years. The extreme improbability of her knowing of Eve's existence weighed as nothing against his faith in her ability to go on disrupting his life. She *pesters* me, he would say. He said it often, because the results of their marital couplings persisted in linking them. The children of his first marriage had not turned out well, and occasions for the parents to confer kept arising. She's *pestering* me again, he would say.

She's a *difficult* woman, his second wife would agree. It was their sole remaining point of agreement. It was a litany with them, and gave the comfort that litanies give. The children of his second marriage had not yet reached the age of disappointment, and he pinned all his hopes on them.

Yes, it was almost certainly his first wife pestering him again.

In which case he was safe.

Unless of course it was his second wife wanting him to think it was his first wife.

These were the complications with which he lived. Some men were lucky, some were not. His thoughts weighed on him like a bruise.

A red light glared and he braked sharply, feeling querulous. What was the point, so late at night, with scarcely any cars on the road? Really, it was ridiculous, and his fingers tapped out a tattoo of irritation on the wheel. Anger, that serpentine virus, went slinking down from his head and along his arms and out to his fingertips which beat time like kettledrums on the . . . his fingers beat time . . . oh no, not again.

By the ghastly light, neon, of the street lamps, he saw his purple hands, his purple wrists, his purple arms. His whole body was a bruise.

In the early stages, his condition was manageable. It was like having an eccentric tic. The colours came and went quite swiftly, as though someone were changing channels or playing with a switch or directing a movie projector at the surface of his skin.

But then days came when a tint would settle in like a stationary weather system. Blue, for instance. Not the peacock blue of passion, but the other one, a glum slate blue.

"It's rare," his doctor told him, "but not unknown." His doctor, it must be ruefully confessed, was rather pleased. All too infrequently did a general practitioner have a chance with the medical journals. "I've had to read up on your condition. Biofeedback research and so on, a whole new area." The medical hands, with their long white fingers, were tented reverently; the medical throat was thoughtfully cleared. "What you are experiencing is a sort of mind-body anxiety loop, more a psychiatric problem actually." The doctor looked tactfully out the window and coughed. "It — ah — arises when the subject has no — ah — appreciable sense of self. When he measures himself by reflected opinion. He *becomes* as it were, that reflection. As he perceives it, that is."

The doctor rose and crossed to the window. "Astonishing thing, the mind." He coughed again, very politely. "Research indicates," he said, looking out at the city, "that subjects are afraid to speak in their own voice. That is to say, they find it necessary to quote an endorser, sometimes even for quite trivial —"

"But . . ." Adam objected fretfully, "my wife used to be a nurse and she says it's just tension, extreme tension, because there was this, ah, awkward situation . . . So she feels, my wife that is, that you should be treating me for stress. She feels you are not taking full account . . . She thinks I should get a second opinion."

"Yes," his doctor said. "I see."

Adam became used to himself as blue. Depression Blue, that is; not the other, not the cobalt of passion. This was a greyish blue, a little bleak perhaps, but inoffensive. People accepted him. Word got about, as word will, that he had a rare blood disease, a sort of late life twist on the "blue baby" syndrome (slowly fatal, alas) and a wise man disdains to interfere with the ship of rumour. Perhaps he placed a judicious hand on the tiller from time to time: to avoid unwarranted sensationalism, any thought of the newest diseases, for example. No, no, it was nothing like that. A hereditary matter, obscure, with a lineage that ran to princelings and czars.

Young women — students — looked at him with eyes full of shock and tears and offered the consolation of their bodies. He's so *chromatic,* they would sigh. And then the blue would go through sea changes, fleeting intensities, turn tinted somersaults. Perhaps the colours themselves would cause the phone to ring in the middle of a pyrotechnic night.

Then the Phases of the Bruise would set in again.

"I don't think I can go on living like this," his wife told him.

"Like what?" he asked with innocent eyes. "What are you talking about?"

You know, replied the fragile silent back of his wife.

"Like what?" he demanded, aggrieved, his belligerence rising. "Like *what?*"

"I'm taking the children," she said, and all colour drained from him in an instant, though his bleached voice babbled on and on. "I promise, I promise, I *promise*, I swear to you that I won't . . ." (He crossed his heart. He kneeled and hugged her legs. He was always obedient. When he was a child he always coloured inside the lines.) "They throw themselves at me," he sobbed. "They compromise me. I'm just being kind and they misinterpret . . ."

The tears ran and ran, a Yangtse of remorse, a yellow river. Yellow settled in for days and moved in him with a slow malarial swell. Everyone thought he had jaundice. He took valium, librium, xanax, and saw white lights with an undershadowing of Depression Blue. Not a happy combination, blue and yellow. He was obliged to wear gloves and sweaters and a cloth hat pulled low over his face.

The Jimmy Swaggart of academe, he overheard one colleague murmur to another, *wearing his true coat of many colours.*

Adam shut his office door and swallowed a couple of emerald capsules (green peace, the doctor had joked) and pulled a bottle of Scotch from a drawer. The room

was full of shifting light. When his head sank onto the
desk, he watched his cheeks bleed colour into the blotting pad. He slept and dreamed.

He was outside in the cold, looking into a candlelit room
where three women played bridge. The chair of the
fourth player was empty, the absentee's cards neatly
ranked in their suits on the table. He could not see the
women clearly, though they all wore black and seemed
pale and delicate as though recently bereaved, and yet
they gave off that golden aura that beautiful women give
off. They touched one another frequently, they leaned
toward one another and smiled, they were animated,
they listened to one another gravely and with an air of
gentle solicitude. He wished he could hear what they
were saying. Perhaps they were sisters. Certainly such a
palpable bond of tenderness linked them that he felt en-
vious. He felt intensely excluded.

The candles — there were scores upon scores of them
— burned brightly. A fire crackled in the grate.
Everything spoke of warmth and welcome, and he
wanted to be invited in. He wanted to play. He wanted
to sit in the empty chair. He rapped on the window and
the women glanced up momentarily but were too ab-
sorbed in the cards to notice him.

He rapped on the glass again, more loudly. He
wanted to know who the missing fourth player was.
"Who's the dummy?" he shouted.

The women raised their heads and looked toward the
window, puzzled. He realised then that he knew them:
hs first wife, his second wife, and Eve; but they gave no
sign of hearing or seeing anyone. He was rapping, rapping, rapping on the glass, his knuckles frantic. "I want
to play with you," he called.

His wives were still as a tableau, waiting. Eve touched

their sleeves gently and pushed back her chair and walked across the room to the window. She opened it and
leaned into the moonless night and the trees.

"Eve," he said gratefully, humbly. "Please let me
in."

Eve looked carefully this way, that way. "Is anybody
there?" she asked.

"Eve," he said, frightened. Their eyes were only inches apart. "Eve! It's me." He felt feverish, he
detonated peacock blue, he sweated cobalt.

Eve blinked and rubbed the back of one hand across
her eyes. "There must be a prism in someone's
window," she said over her shoulder. "It must be turning somewhere."

She closed the casement and went back to the table.
"There's nobody there," she said. He saw her kiss both
of his wives lightly on the forehead, and then the women
picked up their cards and leaned towards each other
smiling, a closed circle.

Dear Amnesty

All the letters — they would have made a snowstorm —
began with *Your Excellency* . . . Sarah always wrote
them by hand, with a fountain pen, taking particular
care with the flourishes: the sensuous f's, the loopy l's,
the trailing lace flounces on the y's. *Your Excellency: It
has come to my attention that contrary to Article
XXIII, Clause 6, subsection iv of your own Constitu-
tion* . . . Her lips were bitten to a bruised purple as she
wrote. Also — and this was beginning to be a problem
— she had to sit on her bed with the goosedown quilt
pulled up to her armpits.

Her son and daughter used to joke about the quilt —
that was when the children still found it a laughing matter. "First sign of arterio-antarcticosis," Richard used
to say. "Commonly referred to as icicles in the
bloodstream." Richard was a second-year Med student;
his head was crammed with biology; he liked to draw
short straight lines between cause and effect. That was
before things got out of hand, before Rosita moved in
and the children moved out again. "You'll progress on
to frozen mucus," Richard promised, "stalactites in the
abdomen, and then Ice Age catatonia. That's when the
shivering stops and they wrap you up in a white
blanket."

Sarah did not laugh. She was deeply embarrassed. She hadn't realised she shivered as she wrote. She put on a sweatshirt and finished her letter.

"Mother!" Katy fumed. "Your sense of humour's iced over already. Completely on the blink. What's *happening* to you?"

Richard asked: "Is all this because of Dad?"

Sarah blinked. When she closed her eyes, she saw blinding asterisks and zigzags: a random geometry of directions changed, fault lines, lifelines, scars, prison bars, the furrows and welts of old wrongs. Some of the lines intersected (there were sparks, the soft pouf of explosions) and some never met.

"After the moment of intersection," she said, "the lives diverge." Further and further. Already their father (had she really been married to him for twenty-five years?) was remote as an asteroid; but she and Rosita lived parallel lives and could not hold hands.

Her son and daughter looked at each other, and the look struck her in passing, a glancing blow. Later, the bruise would form.

"It's odd," she said, "how people only *comment* when the private and the public . . . when outer politics and inner politics, I suppose I should say . . . at those brief interludes, you know, when they become *congruent.*"

"Mother," Katy murmured, cajoling. "Some people can handle this and some can't. I think you should just give money and leave the letters to someone else."

"What you need right now," Richard said, "until you feel more . . . I mean, until you sort out, you know, about Dad . . . You really need to be doing something *upbeat* rather than . . ."

"Perhaps you're right."

"Otherwise," Katy said (she was a first-year Arts student), "I'll have to give up my flat and live here permanently again, so I can keep an eye on you."

"Oh no, really. I'll stop," Sarah promised. She wanted to stop. But she couldn't. She would huddle under the quilt, pretending to read, her shivering muffled in goose-down. *Your Excellency* . . . She kept her fountain pen tucked under the mattress.

In the late afternoons, they sat by the bay window that looked out on the horsechestnut tree. Katy sat cross-legged on the box-seat, the curved part, so that she had a skyful of horsechestnut candles (milky as twists of whipped cream) and the undersides of leaves; Sarah sat on a cushion on the floor, her back against the window box, her head against her daughter's knees.

Katy unpinned her mother's hair and brushed it, languidly, deliberately, a hundred strokes, a thousand strokes.

"Ahh," Sarah purred, "that feels good, so comforting. Do you remember . . .?"

Did Katy remember? When Katy was a little girl, Sarah would brush out her black ringlets (she had her father's colouring, her father's curls), would brush them out one by one, wrapping each around her index finger like a tendril, stroking it with the bristles.

And did Richard remember how she used to stroke his hair while she told him bedtime stories, how she couldn't bring herself to clip his one-year-old curls? his two-year-old . . .? Until his father, outraged, whisked him off to the barber's.

And did her husband remember . . .?

But the past was a Dead Letter Office, a great storehouse of messages never delivered.

Your Excellency, Sarah composed, drafting the next

letter in her mind. *It is not the past history, but the future of your* . . .

She began again: *When you yourself were a child, Your Excellency* . . .

Or maybe: *Perhaps Your Excellency has not realised that the inflicting of pain will destroy your own . . . Present suffering, Your Excellency, can gobble up the entire past, indeed, can swallow time itself* . . .

There it was, the answer to all the riddles, clear as the kernel of a flame: The past did not count; there *was* no past.

"There *is* no past," she says. "There is only the present tense."

Katy pauses in her brushing, a handful of her mother's hair lifted up to the light, and looks at Richard. Richard presses his lips together, folds his book over his index finger, and blinks rapidly. "I'll make you some tea, Mother," he says. Katy holds the hair and runs her brush upwards from the nape of her mother's neck.

Sarah thinks of Rosita's long dark hair, snarled and matted from months in prison. She imagines herself combing it, untangling the wrongs, smoothing out the day's cruelties. She thinks of Rosita's children. Rosita is almost a decade younger than Sarah, but she has ten children. The oldest is nineteen — Katy's age; Sarah sees Rosita's daughter against the light, against the horsechestnut candles, the little ones clinging to her skirt; she is brushing their hair and singing to them.

"It was something I always wanted," Sarah muses, "when I was a child myself . . . To have a little girl with curly hair." She twists her head backwards and up to look at her daughter. She smiles "You're so *unharmed*," she sighs. "So beautiful."

But Katy has not yet discovered this fact. Katy does not believe it. (There is a certain fellow student, male, who never calls; there is her father who finds it "awkward" to call; "for the time being," he has explained, until the young woman he is now living with has time to . . .) Katy insists she is ugly; she says this often with an angry sort of pride.

Oh dear god, *no*, Sarah disputes; you're striking, you're one of a kind, you're very beautiful.

And Richard says: You're OK, kid. Really, you're OK.

Katy wrinkles up her nose and purses her lips. "Sure," she says.

She brushes her mother's hair and fixes her eyes on the creamy candles in the horsechestnut tree.

As soon as Sarah heard the mailman's step on the porch, she would begin to shiver; though this would pass quickly if none of the letters bore the Amnesty logo: a candle in a cage of barbed wire. Today, Sarah would think — and the shadow of a memory of an echo of hope would flit into the morning, would pass like a swiftly flying bird — today there was no one who . . . there was not one single act of . . . not one instance anywhere in the world . . .

But once or twice a week, she was required to write letters. She had to huddle under the quilt and pretend to read.

Katy was upset when letters fluttered out from a pillow on washday. "Mum," she pleaded. "I think you need help, you know? I mean, this is out of control, it's obsessive."

"Yes," Sarah said. She knew it was out of control. She hung her head and sat there meekly, hugging herself for the cold.

"Look," Richard said. "I've been reading up about this, about . . . well, you know, traumatic change, the stress scale, stuff like that. It's called displacement, what you're doing. Well, to some extent we're *all* . . . I mean here we all are, back home, practically *huddling* together . . . It's not unusual, it's even healthy for a while, depending on what you pick as your substitute for . . ."

"Yes," Sarah said, "but the thing is . . ." The thing was, she was one of them now: no outer casing, naked, exposed, waiting for blows. "I know how she feels, so I *have* to help."

"Know how who feels?"

"Rosita Romero. Well, all of them." Though, regardless of country, they had all come to look like Rosita.

"Mother." Richard was disturbed. "I agree that *somebody* . . . But I don't think, right now, this is the kind of thing that you . . ."

"If you read the Urgent Action Bulletins," Sarah said helplessly, "you would understand. In fact, maybe you two —"

"Mum." Katy was pacing, Katy was folding the letters into pellets. "There's such a thing as knowing your own limits. And you and Dad . . . this is not without repercussions for *us*, you know. I don't see . . . these people you write letters for . . . I don't see where they get the right to swallow up our lives."

Sarah watched anxiety pluming around them like a cloud shot through with orange and red. She studied it, fascinated, and realised: There's nothing they can do about it; it's like my shivering.

When she came home from work the next day, Katy's things were gone and there was a note beside the telephone:

Dear Mum: I'm moving back into the flat with San-
dra and Jill. If you need me, call me. Or maybe write,
since you're so good at that. I could do with a few let-
ters of support myself. And so could you, of course.
But I know my limits. Love, Katy.

"I don't know what to do," Richard worried.
"There's this biology project I'm supposed to be working on; it involves a field trip. But how can I leave you
when you're —"

"Oh Richard, don't be silly. It's high time we stopped
— what did you call it? — *huddling* . . . I think you
should move back into residence. And there's nothing
the matter with me. I'm fine."

"But you're not. You're behaving in this . . . it
scares me, it's obsessive."

"I'll stop," she promised, as Richard packed his
things — although she knew it was not within her power
to stop.

Rosita has long dark hair and a tiny mole low on the left
cheek. Sarah's hair is fair-turning-silver, and still hangs
below her shoulders when she unpins it; her mole is near
the right corner of her lips. Each month when Rosita
begins to bleed, Sarah wakes with the sensation of a
leaden ball low in her belly; she reaches down with her
finger, slides it into warm fluids, tastes her own salty
menses.

The night she staggers next door to Mrs Donovan and
is rushed off in an ambulance, Mrs Donovan holds her
hand in the back of the van. "It's a miscarriage," she
says. "Had four myself, in between the six children, so I
know those cramps. Perhaps it's all for the best," she
says, kindly, wiping Sarah's sweating forehead with a
cloth, putting a soothing hand on her jack-knifing
stomach. "So late after the other two. And since he's
left, you know."

"It's Rosita," Sarah grasps between spasms. "It's not a baby, it's Rosita."

At Emergency, they do tests. The interns look at one another and shake their heads and administer sedatives.

"What do men know?" Mrs Donovan says staunchly at her bedside. "Sometimes they slide right down the toilet like a barrel going over Niagara and direct into Purgatory. Little unbaptised souls, not an eye to see them except God's. Don't waste your time expecting doctors to understand. I know women's problems when I see them."

"Yes," Sarah whimpers. Women's problems. "Rosita, Rosita," she whispers into her pillow.

"I've done that, too," Mrs Donovan says. "Gave them all names before they came. Maybe it's tempting fate, I don't know."

"Sympathetic magic," Dr Fisher says. "A form of hysteria. You believe that if you suffer with her, it will help. You believe you are, as it were, draining off some of her pain into your own body."

As a matter of fact, this is exactly what Sarah believes, though she is aware it would not be a good idea to admit it.

"I was baffled at first," Dr Fisher says. "All the signs of an hysterical pregancy. Because you do — don't you? — you do want to believe there's still some physical bond between you and your husband. But your daughter gave me these." Dr Fisher fans out a collection of Urgent Action Bulletins. He reads aloud: *"Rosita Romero, factory worker, province of . . ."*

"Yes, yes," Sarah says impatiently, brushing this aside with her hand.

"Urgent Action: Letters should be sent to His Excellency the —"

"I know," Sarah says. "I did."

Dr Fisher glances at her over his bifocals and continues reading: *"for circulating a petition requesting better conditions at the factory where she works, Rosita Romero was arrested as a 'subversive element'. Evidence gathered from fellow prisoners indicates that Romero was subjected to the 'water torture', in which a hose is inserted into the vagina, and water is admitted under high pressure while an assistant of the interrogator stands on the woman's stomach . . ."*

"I know," Sarah interrupts, doubling over. "You don't have to tell me, I know."

"It's not Rosita Romero's problem you have to work on," Dr Fisher says. "You have to stop avoiding your own. You have to cure your own pain."

Will that lessen Rosita Romero's? Sarah asks herself.

"What do doctors know?" sniffs Mrs Donovan, visiting. "Women's problems. What do doctors know?"

In the middle of the night, Sarah wakes in agony. She is burning and sweating, she seems to be in labour, she feels as though she is giving birth to a wombful of razor blades. Oh God, she moans. She is going to die. She hears groaning and crawls towards it.

"Rosita," she whispers. Rosita's hair is clotted with blood, her face is swollen, she is naked, her body is grotesquely blackened . . . but Sarah recognises her. Doubling over her own pain, pleating it between her knees and breasts, containing it, she cradles Rosita.

She sings to her, she rocks Rosita in her arms, she strokes her hair.

Rosita cannot smile. Her lips are swollen shut, they are purple as eggplants, they are embroidered with scabs of blood. Rosita is slipping away. The mud floor is slick and treacherous, they are both of them sliding downhill. When the guards appear, swinging their truncheons like magicians, like jugglers, like the circus man with one red eye, they take Rosita by the ankles as though she were a sack of dung and begin to heave. It is easy work.

But Sarah digs in her heels and will not let go. She feels the mud and blood squelching up, warm, between her toes. She is on fire from her own contractions, a siren is blaring inside her head. She hooks her arms around Rosita, she sways and weaves to avoid the truncheons, she digs in her heels.

"Let me go," Rosita pleads. Her lips are like rubber pontoons; the words ooze out, slow and viscous. "I can't hold on any more. Let me go," she pleads.

The guards are dragging her off by the ankles. They are using chains; the flesh has gone, Sarah can see the bone.

"Rosita!" she gasps. She is losing her hold, Rosita has almost gone. "Rosita!" She clasps Rosita's hands and hangs on.

All night Sarah braces her legs against the wall. She will not let go. The muscles in her thighs and wrists are fraying like old ropes, they are twisting like knives, they hum a high note of pain so pure it fills the room with fog. Rosita's hands are limp and clammy and slippery as fish. Sarah squeezes harder. She insists that the hands stay warm; she will not let them go.

When morning comes, Sarah wakes exhausted. Her sheets are sodden.

I did not let go, she thinks.

Sarah was curled up on the window-seat looking out at the horsechestnut candles, her daughter visiting for Sunday dinner. Katy sat on a cushion on the floor and leaned against her mother's knees.

"When you were little . . ." Sarah said, winding a black curl around one finger, and stroking it with the brush. She smiled. "Do you remember that time — third grade? fourth grade? — when Michael Dunlap filled your shoes with mud?"

"Oh god, Michael Dunlap!" Katy laughed. "Did he do that? I'd forgotten. I'd completely forgotten. I used to have *nightmares* about that boy." She laughed again then sobered. "Who'd have thought the way things would . . . God, poor Michael Dunlap. What a seesaw life is."

"I saw his mother one day in town. So I asked, you know. Just making small talk, really. It was thoughtless of me. But he's doing all right now, she said. Driving a truck, a fruit and vegetable business, something like that. As a matter of fact, Richard bumped into him one day at a service station on the highway, an incredible fluke, did he tell you? They had a drink together." She ran the brush upwards from Katy's neck, sweeping the curls into clusters; she held them in a loose knot with her left hand, and brushed up again, over and over, massaging.

"Mmmm," Katy purred. She twisted her head back to look at her mother. "Mum?"

"Hm?"

"We're not doing so badly, are we?"

Sarah smiled and feathered the brush in deft little swirls behind Katy's ears.

"Nice," Katy murmured. "Mum?"

"Hmm?"

"Are you still writing those letters?"

"When it's required."

"Do you think it accomplishes anything? Do you ever *hear* . . .?"

"Sometimes." Sarah thought of the terse bulletin that

came . . . oh, two months ago? . . . along with news of fresh arrests in South Korea (please send letters to *His Excellency President Chun Doo-Hwan . . .)* and reports of torture in Iran (please write to *His Excellency . . .)*

Rosita Romero — Update: Released yesterday, after worldwide barrage of letters, and after a number of official and semi-official protests from political figures in the US, Canada, Australia, and Europe. (The politicians themselves were a target of our letter writing campaign.) Released in critical condition, due to several bouts of interrogation with torture. Currently under Red Cross care. Present condition: stable.

"You never hear much," Sarah said. She let Katy's curls fall loose over her shoulders, and ran the brush through them again.

"Don't stop," Katy murmured.

"I had no intention of stopping."

Eggshell Expressway

"Up there," he says, "right up there in the sixth floor window of the book depository, at the very time the supposed sniper had his telescopic sights on the motorcade leaving Kirribilli House and coming over the Harbour Bridge, at the very moment he was allegedly waiting for it to reach the turn in the expressway, at the very second he reportedly fired the shot heard round the world, right up there behind that sixth-floor window — see it? see it? — a very tawdry little scene was taking place.

"Yes," he says, breathing hard. "The Prime Minister's real assassin, the slut herself, was down on her knees between the rifleman's straddled legs. Oh, she set him up all right. He was an innocent, he was duped. Very busy with her tongue, she was; blue in the face, stuffed with it, practically choking."

"Like this?" asks Lisa, busy with her tongue.

"Yes," he moans, "oh dear God, yes. Making sure he'd be caught with his pants down, caught with a smoking gun, hah hah, the little slut. Of course, she'll die for it, she'll hang for it. Jack Ruby is coming to get her, oh God, oh Christ, he's coming, he's coming, he's coming."

"Shh," Lisa mumbles, soothing him, crooning to him with her hands, her mouth. She swallows egg white, salt jelly, yuck, don't blink, don't think, don't puke, don't think. "Don't think about her," she murmurs. "Don't worry about her, everything's gonna be all right."

"A tawdry set-up." He's weeping now. "Taking advantage. Meanwhile the real marksmen (who knows how many?) are everywhere: the toll booth, Circular Quay, the Law Courts, every doorway in King's Cross, the expressway underpass, oh yes, the underpass, that surprises you, doesn't it? You'd be sick at what goes on in that labyrinth, that slime-pit, that sewer-maze, that —"

"Shh," Lisa says, cradling him, her back against pillows. "They missed. They didn't get him."

"They got him," he moans. "They got him." He sees the skull burst like an eggshell, blood all over the expressway.

Shiv knocks on the door. "Time," he grunts. "Hurry up in there, I got someone else waiting."

"I have to get dressed now, Groucho," Lisa says. "You have to go." Sometimes she calls him Groucho; he calls her Old Mole. *Old!* she says; that'll be the day. Eighteen, she says when asked, though she's only fifteen, the age of all the wide world's daughter. This fact is pertinent and she will usually admit it later, sometime before they leave, because she knows what they want and she knows what will bring them back.

"Your fucking time's *up*," shouts Shiv, bang bang on the door.

"Oh, the tollman." Bitter Groucho puts on his trousers. "The tollman, is it? Come for payment in cash and blood. Can't get out of the underpass without paying dearly, can we?"

"Shh," Lisa murmurs, doing up buttons for him. "Shush now." Sometimes she calls him the Underpass Man. Things have come to a pretty underpass, haven't they? he is always and acidly asking. At Ebony's, he means. By any name, a slime-pit is what Ebony's is, he's right about that. If she's with someone new, really new, an American tourist say, she has to warn them. Look, she'll say, don't spin out when we get to the top of the stairs, okay? The joint's a slime-pit. Just close your eyes and don't think, she'll say. It's not so bad once you're inside the room.

She's seen them spin out, but. She's seen them practically puke from the sight of that upstairs hallway. Sweet Jesus, they say, and they want her to come back to the Sheraton, the Hilton, the Sebel Townhouse, wherever, which is nicer, God you wouldn't believe how much nicer, but then you're in heck with Shiv and it isn't worth it. Be out on your backside fast if Shiv loses his cut.

"Who was the bald bloke?" asks Shiv the Divine, the bearer of angel dust. "He looks familiar."

"Yeah, well." Lisa gets out her spoon and crosses it with her lighter, her hands are shaking. "He's a regular."

(Beneath her window, the priest from St Canice's is telling someone about the Halfway House, the de-tox centre, Father Rescue-the-Perishing, he never quits, but St Canice's is okay, she's been there, they treat you decent, give you a decent meal.)

Shiv frowns. "No, I mean . . . he's a fucking VIP, I think. Seen his picture in the paper, or something." Lisa's hands are shaking. "What's he do?"

Under the silver spoon, the flame wavers and dies, Lisa's hands are dancing, *Help me, Shiv,* Lisa's hands are having convulsions. (By the fountain of El Alamein, a circle forms. *At the cross, at the cross,* the Salvation Army sings to the dark, *where I first saw the light . . .)*

Lisa sees light, too much of it, her hands are out of control.

Quick, quick, have mercy O Lord for whom not a sparrow falls to the ground but thou knowest, quick quick under blood where all the hypodermics meet, quick quick, on the wings of a powder-white dove, be swift O Lord, be swift Father Shiv for I have taken the habit, I have sinned, quick quick . . . ahhh, ahhhhhh . . . ahhmen, ahhhmen, aaahhhhhhhhhhmen.

"What's he *do?*" Shiv asks, impatient, touching cigarette glow to flesh. *(Fuck 'em, fuck 'em, ya gotta let 'em know who's boss, ya gotta crack the whip.)*

Lisa opens her eyes very wide, then closes them. She smiles. Slowly, she brings the sleepwalking index finger of her left hand toward the small scorched circle on her right wrist. She strokes it, wondering, and lifts drowsy lids. "It's beautiful, Shiv."

"What the fuck does he do?"

"Who?" Her eyelids flutter and droop. "What does who do?"

"The bald bloke. What the fuck *is* he?"

"Oh him. I dunno. A judge or something, I think. Can't remember."

"Seen his picture in the paper," Shiv says. "Some hanky-panky, it's on the tip of me mind, it'll come to me."

It's his turn again. Groucho's turn.

When it's his turn, he orders the streets to be cleared, he has a day-long curfew. It's in the people's best interests, he says, because of the snipers.

Lisa says: "I can't just stay here, Groucho. I gotta get back to the street, I'm *working*."

But Groucho insists. "I'll pay again." He beams thoughts at her: Get back to your sewer, Old Mole; get back to your tunnels, stay down in your underpass maze.

He's fond of her, he doesn't want her shot down. He offers what protection he can. Not lacking in gentleness or a sense of justice, he has tried to explain that there are rules, good rules, and that the rules must be obeyed because they are in fact immutable, they form a kind of eternal monument that towers above the underpass. Transgressors will be shot down, that is one of the rules, and that explains why she must stay with him. Otherwise the snipers may get her.

Sometimes he comes before it is even dark and pulls down the blinds. "They can't see us in the underpass," he says. "It's black as slime in here."

Sometimes he strings half-hours together like beads, at eighty dollars a shot. Shiv knocks, Groucho pays, Shiv goes. It's fine by Lisa who wears her habit like a nun, the zeal of Ebony's eating her up, six tricks a day, rain or shine, six tricks a day keeps convulsions away. And the tunnels are endless, Groucho says.

"What's his name?" Shiv asks.

Lisa shrugs. "Dunno. I call him Groucho."

"It'll come back to me," Shiv tells her. "I know I seen him in the papers. It'll come back to me who he is, Mr Humpty Dumpty."

He (Mr Humpty Dumpty) considers her territory dark and unmapped. Once, on the bench during session, he wrote and wrote, covering juridical pages in a hand-writing that was spidery, crabbed perhaps, the fountain pen slanted just so. He used the finest of nibs. (Long ago, very young among the boarders with their blazers and ties and terrible sobbing dreams, his penmanship had been deemed worthy of special commendation. There had been a pennant for calligraphy. If I might read the handwriting on the wall, Brother Damian had joked, this is but the first rung of what will be a distinguished career.) *Ebony's Ebony's Ebony's Ebony's,* he wrote on page after page, evidence that might be used against him.

He considers her territory shady, and there are stronger words that he does not say, words that rise into his mouth and cause him discomfort, nausea even. *Disreputable. Murky. Fuzzy. Crotch-ety.* He coughs, and spits the words into a handkerchief already full of some milky viscous substance, and stuffs the handkerchief discreetly into a pocket. On his turf, everything is out in the open and above board. Sharp distinctions come under his jurisdiction. He marks out the boundary lines.

Hup, hup, hup, go the boundary lines, keeping dotted formation, defiling by (when they get down to her, they're defiled, how now Old Mole?), merrily merrily marching through parallax errors, hyphenations, the presenting of arms, all wending their way down past the golden eggshell wall to the underpass.

He pinpoints the risks: the dotted lines, as a fortification system, are intermittent at best. There are constant perforations, imperfections, perfumed slits, perfervid gaps for a quick perv where sewer gas might seep through. He has spoken of the need for constant moral vigilance. Civilisation, that great spreading oak, has root rot, its fruits are infested, the young saplings are diseased, they breed disease, they breed like rabbits, like vermin, like mould in the underpass, even the lamp posts sprout ovaries, and it behoves men of classical education and impeccable parts, men of upright parts, to stand in the mud, sire, to draw the snipers. Ramparts have been called for, a buttressing of the eggshell wall itself, a better fornication policy.

"The perfect legal contract," he confides to a distinguished colleague, "would be constructed so intricately and so exactly that an improper word or thought or interpretation could not find a way in. Or if it did get in, it would vanish, it would never be seen again."

"Ahhh . . . yes," his colleague murmurs. "Quite so."

From under the crimped platinum curls, he (Mr Humpty Dumpty) describes how the contractual labyrinth itself would stir at the first sign of infection, how the coiled sentences would sway and unfurl their darting tongues, how they would swallow the blight whole, ingest it, eliminate it. Illegal words (and thoughts and deeds) would falter, bemazed, they would slide down perfect clauses to the mouth of the minotaur.

On the bench, during session, he draws up meticulous blueprints. His model is the human brain itself, those delicate yolky spirals held in by a tissue of self as thin as eggshell.

"It's a sobering thought," he says to his colleague. "The complexity and the fragility of the mind. Did you know, for example, that if we are prevented from dreaming, we go mad?"

In the underpass, he says into the darkness: "What do you dream about, Old Mole?"

And Lisa answers: "No one at Ebony's has dreams."

"I dreamed," he says, "that the Prime Minister and Princess Diana were leaving Kirribilli House in a black limousine. Princess Di was wearing an off-the-shoulder off-white ball gown that was spattered with the Prime Minister's blood. There were broken eggshells all over the front of the car."

"It means you think Princess Di plays around," Lisa says.

Groucho mournfully demurs. "It means treachery. It means the snipers are out."

Lisa asks: "Shiv, do you ever dream?"

"I never *sleep*," Shiv snaps. "Got no time, I'm a working man. Hurry it up, will ya?"

She is cutting his hair. He watches both of them in the wardrobe mirror.

"If you had three wishes, Shiv, what would you wish?"

"Got no time for guff like that," growls Shiv.

"But if you did have time, Shiv, what would you wish?"

"Oh shut up," he says, hitting her across the mouth with the back of his hand.

Lisa kneads the back of his neck, the way he likes. Lisa kneads and kneads. She wonders: If he asks me what would I wish, will I say "No more cigarette burns"?

Shiv says: "I been taking photographs of you and the bald bloke, the judge, Humpty Dumpty." Lisa's hands hang motionless above the shoulderblades of Shiv. "Don't let on," he says. "I reckon there's money in it. Get on with the haircut, will ya?"

Lisa's hands hover with scissors and comb. Shiv watches her in the mirror. "He ever tell you anything?" Shiv asks.

"Who?"

"You know who I mean. The one I know I seen something about in the papers, but I can't remember what. Could be a few years back. I think he went in for politics or something. He tell you anything?"

*   *   *

"Nah. Only his dreams," Lisa says.

Half hour by half hour, he pays and pays. Lisa hardly has to do a thing, it's easy work. She lies there naked, he strokes her, he talks; in the last few minutes, she has to swallow him, that's it. Up until then, he just talks.

"Where did you go to school, Old Mole?" he asks. "Which convent?"

"I didn't go to a convent, I went to Parramatta State."

"Were the nuns kind to you? Or did they beat you? Did they cover your little buttocks with scars?" He rolls her over to look. "Oh poor little, poor little mole."

(Click, click, goes the camera shutter behind the mirror. In the next room, Shiv watches through one-way glass.)

"There weren't any nuns," she says. "I got those scars from me dad, he drank too much."

"I'll lick them better," he promises. "But you must have been a naughty girl."

"Yeah," she sighs. "I reckon. I got sent to reform school."

"Time," Shiv says, rapping on the door.

("There's money in this," Shiv has told Lisa. "If we get the photographs to the right person, maybe to the Prime Minister himself, I gotta think. Then we show some reporter, or threaten to show . . . I read about something like this once, you can make a fortune.")

Shiv bangs on the door and Groucho pays.

The verdict is "Guilty as charged" and His Honour (Mr Humpty Dumpty) hands down the maximum sentence allowed under law.

"And we cannot stress too much," he says, "that these practices are a rip in the very fabric of society. We cannot send out too strong a signal."

In the Law Courts Club, over Scotch, conscious that not all his colleagues agree with him, conscious that some find him unduly harsh, conscious that some are out to get him, he says passionately: "If we can save only one of those little girls, just one, I'd consider myself . . ."

"They don't last long," a colleague says. (Is he for or against?) "I read that the average lifespan at the Cross, once they're hooked, is five years. Most of them are dead by the time they turn twenty." (Is it a trap? a subtle attack?)

"Awful," His Honour equivocates, in anguish. "Appalling. An expressway to hell. We cannot send out too strong a signal. If I had one wish . . ."

"If you had one wish," Groucho asks Lisa, "what would you —?"

"Sleep," she says. "That's what I'd wish. I wish I could sleep for a week. See, at Ebony's, we never. They charge us thirty dollars a night, but you can't get a bed till after four, then they kick you out at nine in the morning."

"That's appalling," Groucho strokes the tiny golden hairs on her stomach, working down, very slowly, to the underpass. "Where do you go?"

"Nowhere. On the street. Maybe sit in the park till the cops come. You gotta stand, mostly, lean on shop windows."

"Poor little mole," he says. He rolls her over to inspect her scars. "But you've been such a naughty girl."

"Yeah," Lisa shrugs. "I reckon. Hey, guess what, I did have a dream, did I tell you? Well, it wasn't a dream, not really, because I was awake, but it was like a dream. I was on the street, leaning up against a window,

I was feeling good, well naturally, I'd just juiced up, and this . . . this *place,* I saw this place inside my mind. It was a room that no one could get to, except me. There were, like, circles and circles of hedges and no one could find me. I slept for days and days, and Shiv couldn't knock on the door. That's what I'd wish for. Hey, is something the matter? Groucho?''

Oh the pain. He holds his skull between his hands as though it might break.

"Don't spin out," she says, cradling him against her breasts. "Shush now, everything's all right."

"I'm going to buy the whole night for you," he says desperately. "I'm going to buy the whole night, so you can sleep. I'll watch over you while you sleep."

"Groucho," she says roughly, "Groucho . . ." She looks into the mirror and away. She sits over him, knees nipping his waist, and bends low. "Listen," she whispers against his ear. "I'm gonna tell you something I shouldn't ought to. Don't come back here. Shiv's been taking pictures."

"Oh," he says, his head in his hand from the pain.

"It's come to me," Shiv says. "The thing I was trying to remember."

Lisa's hands are shaking. "Hurry, Shiv."

"Knew I'd seen his picture, except it wasn't him after all, musta been his double, this was a coupla years back. He's the dead spit of the one I was thinking of, but. The dead spit."

Hurry, Shiv.

"This other one, he was a judge too, can you beat that? and a dead ringer for Humpty Dumpty, he blew his brains out in a car right on the Cahill Expressway. Right by the underpass. Tow truck comes for this breakdown, and there's a fucking corpse in it with a busted skull. Coupla years back, though, and afterwards it comes out in the papers, dirty pictures, blackmail, the works. That's what give me the idea in the first place. I already made our contacts, I sent our photos, piece'a cake. There's big money coming."

Hurry, Shiv, hurry Shiv, ahhhhhhhhh . . .

"I'll tell ya what's weird though," Shiv says. "When I saw the photos I took, that's when I remembered who he is. Who I thought he was. I seen the pictures before, in the papers."

Lisa smiles a beatific smile.

"The dead spit, the dead bloody . . . Hey!" Shiv says. "Hey! Shit, that's *my* stuff, what the hell are you . . . you'll o.d., you stupid bitch, what the hell are you doing?"

Lisa smiles a slow-motion smile. Beyond the underpass, she can see the circles and circles of privet and the room that no one can reach.

To Be Discontinued

"Randomness," he says, nodding vigorously and taking a large gulp at the same time, and Katharine watches with a kind of anguished fascination as the word splashes against his teeth and lips and disperses itself along the seams of his eighty years. He looks at the glass, puzzled, and brushes at the spreading wet circle on his shirt and jacket. "How . . .?" he mumbles. It is as though he has seen dampness well up from his chest to stain him.

"And . . . and indeterminancy," he says, frowning, losing the tail-end of an idea. He studies his soaked clothing, squinting down at it, adjusting perspective. A thought finds him. "Before the war, '32 was it? I'd just arrived. Dazed, you can imagine; wandering round . . . wandering? floating, I should say, the hick from Nova Scotia thinking *Princeton, Princeton!* and I bump into him just like that. I mean, collide. The eyes, the hair turning handsprings, you couldn't mistake . . . My god! I thought, *Einstein."*

He pronounces it *deutsch*ly, lovingly, savouring the moment: *Ein-shtein*. And Katharine sees New Jersey before the fall, the campus-green Eden, white spires, orange papery trees; she smells September-crisp air that carries not a trace, not a whiff of Hitler. Is it possible to believe in such a time? A fiction surely, pure mythos. Hitler will be, and is, and always was.

"Kann you tell me Einstein says to me" — and the accent is mock shtammer and Teutonic spume — *"Kann you tell me, ver iss I am?"*

They both laugh, o wonderful, wonderful, she says, and did you really? as he is resting a hand on her knee, collide?

"Collisions," he says. "Random collisions. I've always maintained they are the essence, if indeed randomness can be said to have an essence . . . if indeed it were possible to pin down such a concept as . . . but since the very first novel I've . . ." He is patting her knee with staccato agitation, as though he were drumming on a lectern. "They've let it go out of print, you know," he tells her suddenly, leaning forward and slopping wine over both of them. "Oh dear oh dear," he sighs.

"Really, it's nothing, I do it to myself all the time." She dabs at her skirt, his sleeve, with a cocktail napkin. (Will I tell this sometime? she wonders. The way he speaks of Einstein?) Nothing but uneasiness arises from the thought. It feels improper, this towering over him, perched on the arm of a sofa into which he is pleated like a shrinking origami trick, a paper crane folding its wings, say; or a bonsai oak growing smaller and smaller. Ta-ra-rum, ta-ra-rum, he is drumming on her knee, and she sees, horrified, and then wills herself not to see, convinces herself she has not seen, the tears on his cheeks.

Last time he was here, she thinks, ten years ago, it was the Great Hall; this time a small lecture room.

"Oh I've *always* . . ." A young student who pushes hanks of curls off her face regards him raptly. "I've *always* wanted to meet you . . . such a wonderful

speech." And "Unforgettable, sir, absolutely unforgettable," says a hearty voice, beardless but with chest hair
showing through its open-necked shirt. "We met back
in '80 when you came to . . . a distinctive voice, you
were kind enough to say, and since then as a matter of
fact . . ." Always wanted, and What an honour, and
Your books have always . . . other students murmur,
pressing adoration and title pages for the signing ʋpon
him.

Katharine sees him plump up in the sofa, like a wilting
narcissus that has been watered.

"I do not believe," he announces in a sudden access
of lucid energy, "I do not believe that the current course
of the novel can be further pursued. Mere anarchy is
loosed upon . . . and must have its day, I suppose."

He strokes the cheek of the nearest student as he
hands back her book. "But then it is the task of
language, the task of narrative, to *connect* the random
events, to divine the . . . Where is the novel of ideas?
Where is the thunder of language? Where is
the . . . What did you say your name was, my dear?"

At the windowsill, Katharine looks out into the campus,
not Princeton, but with much the same lawns, crab-
apples in bloom, lilacs, no white spires however. Here
the buildings are limestone, stolid grey, though greened
and softened with obligatory ivy, indeed so extravagantly softened that whole walls undulate in the breeze.
There's a lake beyond the massy horsechestnuts. Campus pastoral, hasn't someone called this? (When?
Where? Which country? In a letter perhaps?) It is late
evening, but floodlights cast a golden twilight.

She is watching the back of the biology building,
waiting. And there, yes, the girl appears again, crossing
the courtyard from the library, wheeling her bicycle,

pushing it into the gap in the privet behind the biology building, hiding it. The book-bag causes her indecision: should she leave it in the bicycle basket? take it with her? She hooks it over one shoulder, smooths shorts and t-shirt with her free hand, tosses back her long hair. She stands at the locked rear fire-escape door which can only be opened from the inside. Open sesame, she whispers. No, of course she does nothing of the kind. She transfers the book-bag to left hand and shoulder, scoops up a handful of pebbles and tosses them at a third floor window.

Up there, the drapes part for a moment, then close again. Katharine counts to thirty (five seconds for the hallway, ten for summoning the elevator, five for each floor) and the rear door of the biology building opens. Is it the courtyard light, puddling into the door, that makes him shade his eyes, look up and opposite swiftly? He steps out as though for the evening paper, a middle-aged man, professorial, rumpled. The girl hugs him. They disappear into the building.

"Penny for them," says a colleague at her elbow, setting his drink on the windowsill.

"God, Jim, don't *do* that."

"Sorry. Didn't mean to startle you." Jim leans against the moulding and yawns. "These tedious old monuments."

She raises her eyebrows. "Do you mean me? Or the great man?"

"Whom do you think? Rather past it, isn't he? Poor old sod. Speech all over the shop."

Why does this hit her like a punch, make her angry, make her want (oh for Christ's sake!) to cry? She says, determined to keep her voice casually level: "I thought he was wonderful."

"Women!" Jim laughs, patting her on the head.

"Sentiment, sentiment, every time. To tell you the truth, Kate, even in his heyday I found his novels turgid and rambling. But a monument is a monument. Where's Robert tonight? Toronto for the Learned Societies? Or the Montreal thing?"

"Neither. Deep in proofreading and compiling the index."

"Ah. Mary's got a School Board meeting. Shall we cut loose and go for drinks at Schooner's?"

"Thanks. Maybe some other time."

"Sure," he says curtly. "Think I'll get some more Scotch while they're laying it on."

From the windowsill, she watches the pale yellow square on the third floor opposite, the drapes drawn but backlit by a desk lamp. She sees the car pull up in University Avenue at the front of the biology building, sees the middle-aged woman get out, sees her press the night-bell by the carved oak doors, casually, not thinking of anything in particular, a routine matter, picking someone up. And the watcher at the windowsill imagines giving this picture to students in a writing class: What is the relationship between the three people: the man, the girl, the woman with the car? What will happen next?

Something of the sort was done at Harvard, she recalls, with startling results. Two control groups, one male, one female, were shown a picture: a tranquil river scene, a wooden bench near a low bridge, a couple sitting close together on the bench. The women, Radcliffe women, the best and the brightest, saw love love love, with possible probable eventually almost certain loneliness lurking somewhere in the wings, beneath the bridge, behind the bench. But the men, more than twenty percent of the men, leaders of the future, those culturally favoured and civilised Harvard men saw homicide, suicide, jealousy, stabbing, kidnapping, rape. Conclusion of the dazed researchers: intimacy is fraught with violence in male fantasies.

She turns from the window and sees Jim setting down two empty glasses, his own and that of a student, the one with the hanks of curls and the pale pink t-shirt. Something has been decided between them, they are about to leave. Jim glances across the room, catches her eye (important to him, that, she realises), and throws her an ambiguous half-belligerent look that she interprets as: *Your loss, sweetie.* In response, she raises a non-committal eyebrow and her glass.

She looks out the window again and the woman ringing the night-bell has disappeared. Someone has pushed the buzzer that will unlock the doors for ten seconds (but was it the man behind the third floor window? Or a random response to buttons randomly pushed? Does the man in the third floor office know the woman is rising through the elevator shaft?) From deep in the privet comes a small metallic gleam: the courtyard light bouncing off the bicycle guard. The watcher sets down her empty glass on the windowsill, fishes for her car keys, and leaves while all possibilities remain open.

In the parking lot, she stands distracted by the perfume of . . . lilacs? Is it? Or something tropical: magnolia, jasmine? There's a dark splash either of hibiscus or Icelandic poppy. Why is she here? She looks at her car keys uncertainly and puts them in her pocket. Something, the fog that comes off water on summer nights, pulls her; she follows it, dropping below the campus buildings, down the green slope to the banks. Brisbane River, yes, St Lucia campus: things click into place.

Another reprimand for an imperfect recitation of

Verlaine, it still smarts, the evening tutorial session in shards behind her. Why does the old ogre — ogress? — find them necessary, these public bombardments of scorn? The girl, bruised, turns and looks back up the sweep of lawn to the cloisters, watching. It is said that the dragon lady paces round the grounds at night, academic gown billowing, reading Proust aloud to herself: Edwina Waterhouse who has terrorised and taught every known Queenslander French (so it sometimes seems). Crazy old bitch, the girl murmurs savagely to herself.

But then, even at this moment, she forgives all — every Queensland student forgives all — because of EW's passion, because of fleeting visitations of vulnerability, because Edwina is such an endless generator of anecdotes: the real thing, the eccentric-in-residence.

There was the time, late afternoon, on a walk through the cloisters from the library, head down, deep in thought, and here was — gulp — too late to avoid her, Edwina. Simone de Beauvoir, wasn't it? or Colette or maybe Françoise Sagan, or all three, who held Edwina in their wry and passionate grip for that particular half hour. And why, why *au nom du ciel?* had a student of hers not read, *incroyable!* had actually not read . . . *Vraiment?* the latest Françoise Sagan. *Incroyable!* Not on the course had *rien, rien à faire* with the matter!

And then chalk-dusted black-gowned Virginia-Woolfish Edwina reached up with a hand on the path of a vivid thought; felt by accident the bun that lay loosely on the nape of her neck, untidy, like an improperly annotated footnote. Caesura. A break in the brisk weather of conversation that scudded by in inscrutable French blusters. With both hands, Edwina gathered up a web of the thickish tendrils that trailed across her shoulders, was brisk with her hairpin-fishing fingers, twisted, tightened, got things settled. And then, with ever-after-to-be-wondered-at plaintiveness, asked: *"Pourquoi ne m'avez-vous pas dit que j'étais décoiffée?"*

"Parce que, ma professeur très honorée", her speechless student could not even stammer, "because I am terrified of you."

And who could have believed you cared a jot about the state of your hair?

Crazy old bitch, the girl by the river thinks fondly, remembering. By the boathouse she rummages under the bougainvillea for her bicycle, looks at her watch one more time. He's not coming tonight then. Some days nothing goes well. Will he ever come again? Did she dream him? Can she pass French? Is she stupid? Who can expect happiness to last?

She pushes her bicycle up the slope which is of course endless, which runs all the way uphill into past and future like Escher's waterwheel and begins again again begins again. Again: this is a forlorn ritual, pleasurably painful. She will wheel the bicycle through the crescent of cloisters just in case, though he has never . . . and cycle home past King's College looking up at his lighted window.

Through the cloisters a shadow moves towards her . . . no? yes, over there where the oleanders huddle darkly. No. Though there *is* someone coming from the direction of King's . . . a speck, a mist, a shape, I wist. I wished, I wish, she sighs. Pathetic. I place him everywhere.

"My god," he says, slamming into nothing. "It's really you, it's *you*, I was afraid I was, I thought for sure I'd have missed you, didn't think I had a *hope* . . . We had a speaker after High Tea, I couldn't get away."

She squeezes her hands tightly around the bicycle grips — this is not really happening, she knows it — then slides them along to the cool and rational metal.

"You look as though you've seen a ghost," he teases. A hand brushes her cheek, light as air, and for a dizzy second she has a vision of the essence of things: the whole Queensland quad a shimmering cotillion of electrons.

Particles, photons, neutrinos, the fizz and bounce of them, the dip of years, the curve of time, she has to blink. And how did they get down to the bank again?

Even in June, the Lake Ontario water chills.

She dries her feet on the grass, puts her sandals back on, looks around for her bicycle. Gone too? She stands frowning, jingling the car keys in her hand. Where did I park?

In front of the biology building, she leaves the hazard lights flashing, rings the night-bell. There's a long wait, no answering buzz, perhaps he's gone. She pushes a number of buttons at random, with no luck. Here we go round *ah the years, the years*, she thinks, turning on the ignition. But wait, he's there, he's breathless, chasing the car, rapping on her window, yes it's   it *is*, it *is*.

"God," he says (in the car, lights off, engine still running) his mouth and tongue on her shoulders her throat, his fingers combing her hair. "I've been waiting all evening, I was . . ." (Are they laughing or crying?) When breath comes back to them, she turns the ignition off, he says: "My daughter dropped by without warning. I was afraid she'd never leave, I was afraid you'd come and go." He rubs the back of one hand across his eyes. "I was afraid she'd see you."

Her smile is sardonic; no, imitation sardonic; for what does she, so recklessly happy, care? "And this would be worse than if your wife . . .?"

Silly question, she thinks, since it's the last thing, surely, that anyone lets go. A universal need, perhaps: to preserve, to tend and water the illusion that in our children's eyes we are faultless.

"I've only got fifteen minutes. Twenty at the most," she says. "My son needs the car, he's got a nightshift job for the summer."

"How was the great man?"

"Poignant. Rummaging through the new physics, like everyone else. You would have liked it, I think. He quoted someone who says that memory's holographic. Distributed, not localised. Nudge a frequency, you get the thing back entire, the whole replay."

He takes her hand, sucks her fingers one by one, delicately, dropping a line between each knuckle: *"Clocks and carpets and chairs,"* he murmurs,

On the lawn all day,
And brightest things that are theirs . . .
Ah, no; the years, the years . . .

Wondering, delighted, she asks: "How do *you* know Hardy?"

"Surprise, surprise. Even illiterate scientists read from time to time."

"Oh!" she says sharply. "Look. There he is." A frail man, elderly, is wandering beneath the lilacs. "It's him. He must have lost his bearings. They've given him a room in Vic Hall. Shall we go and . . .?"

Watching him stumble, sway a little, gaze vaguely about, they cannot bring themselves to . . . what? *expose* him. They stand in the courtyard, discreetly close, forearms brushing, and wait. Transgressors. Eventually the old man tacks toward them, squinting. "In '32?" he queries, plaintive. "Yes." He steadies the question, nodding. "I didn't know up from down, just wandering round thinking *Princeton, Princeton* when all of a sudden my god I thought *Einshtein* . . .''

Reverently — yes, you could call it reverence — they guide him toward Vic Hall. Can you tell me, she thinks of asking the girl at the night desk, the great man, her lover, can you tell me ver iss we are?

The Loss of Faith

His first wife was living in Sydney when she died, and on that very day Adam saw her on the subway in New York. He was just getting off the Broadway Local at Times Square, and trying to find the place where you go down the stairs for the crosstown shuttle to Grand Central, when they collided.

"My God," he said. "Faith!"

For whole seconds he felt his waking vertigo (Adam's dreams wore bells and motley, they were extravagant, their sense of humour was decidedly off-kilter) and dizziness nipped at his brain like a terrier. He thought he could hear a phone ringing; yes, he definitely heard the descant "pips" that signal a long-distance call in Australia. The conviction that he must have been changing trains at Circular Quay instead of in Manhattan was so intense that he saw the Sydney sky, very blue, and the Harbour Bridge, right there against the subway pillars. There was, in fact, a travel poster (Paul Hogan grinning, the bridge, the opera house, *G'day, mate, come and see us Down Under for the Bicentennial);* and so later he thought that this was the explanation; until later again when his daughter Robbie (the eldest of his three children, the one who forgave him least) phoned with the news of Faith's death. But for twenty-four hours or so, he thought the travel poster was the explanation.

"Faith," he murmured, dazed, unable to move, while Paul Hogan smirked in peripheral vision and Times Square seethed above their heads.

Faith looked young and quite lovely — the way she had looked in their halcyon years — but very pale.

"Keep your hands to yourself, mister," she said in a flat Bronx accent, and someone shoved him aside and next thing he knew he was in the vast rococo barn of Grand Central Terminal with thousands of people milling around and a horrible sensation — a sort of rising fog of queasiness moving on up from his ankles — that he was going to faint. Air, he thought, *air*, trying to grope his way out to Forty-second Street but getting lost in the tunnels and turning into the Oyster Bar instead.

"Table, sir?" A waitress laid her hand lightly on Adam's arm and he nodded. She was blond and mechanically flirtatious. "Will anyone be joining you, sir? No? This way then."

It was murky as sin in the Oyster Bar, and he tripped over several pairs of feet. On his table a feeble glow of candle was drowning itself, swamped in paraffin. He gulped down two beers (Foster's, thanks to the ubiquitous Mr Hogan) and told himself: *It doesn't mean anything, seeing Faith's double. It doesn't mean anything at all.* But the trouble with a Marist Brothers education — Sydney, circa late '40s, early '50s — was that the world was always thick with symbol. You could never escape it.

"It means something," he told the blond waitress lugubriously.

"It's just the wax," she said. "See, if you tip it, you can free the wick again."

"What?"

"See? I've relit your candle."

Fat chance, Adam thought. "My first two wives," he said solemnly, "were Australian." He studied the palms of his hands, seeking clues to a mystery. He raised his head and listened to something far away. "Is that a telephone ringing?"

She smiled. "Would you care to order now?"

"And so am I," he said. "Australian. Still." He frowned and added: "I think."

"I recommend the Oysters Florentine."

"If I'm anything," he amended, taking hold of her wrist and mournfully running an index finger up and down the soft inner skin of her forearm. "I'm not from New York."

"Who is?"

"I get down from Northampton — Northampton, Mass — once or twice a —"

"Don't tell me." The waitress rolled up her eyes in mock despair. "You teach at Smith."

"Well yes, as a matter of . . . How'd you —?"

"I'm a Smithie. Class of '84. But you weren't . . ."

"No. I went there in '85. What's a nice Smith girl doing —"

"Working her way through grad school. Columbia."

"Columbia." He sighed heavily and rested his hands, palms up, on the table. "I was at Columbia when . . ." He pondered the zigzag of his marriage line, hanging onto the tail of a thought. "I'll tell you something weird: I only get down to the Big Apple once or twice a year, but something bloody strange happens every time. I think it's because —"

"Listen," she said awkwardly. "I'll come back in —"

"— I associate New York with guilt. That's why it happens."

"— back in ten minutes, okay? When you're ready to order."

"What's your name?" he asked, pulling the inside of her wrist to his lips.

"Sandra," she said. Oh damn, she thought. She was an absolute sucker for a man with tears in his eyes. This was on account, so sundry therapists assured, of her feckless father who'd moved on and moved on, as one day Sandra herself might be able to do. But for now she was stuck (though improving). For now, she would go as far as drinks and sex (providing he was willing to play safe) but not in her apartment, and not more than once, because she knew him already. He'd had a sad life, he favoured clingy and insecure women, she was not — she refused to be — his type.

"I've had a sad life," Adam sighed.

I am not I am not thank God his type, Sandra told herself, running through her therapist's catechism. I will not be a breast for one more child-man to suck, I am cured of congenital soft-heartedness, I am definitely learning not to . . . "I get off in two hours," she said. "If you want to talk."

"My third wife," Adam told her as they lay side by side in his hotel bed, "well not wife, strictly speaking, we never married . . . but she was American, a therapist."

A therapist, Sandra thought. It figures.

"We met on my sabbatical here in New York."

"At Columbia," she said.

"Right. Columbia." Nineteen seventy-six, that year of flags and tall ships, of academic excitement, marital chaos, erotic trysts, the smell of hotel sheets — it came back to him with the faint sweetness of perfume left on a sweater. "My second wife was dreadfully unhappy," he sighed. "In New York, I mean. It's very difficult to live with someone as unhappy as that, someone who is so *desperately* . . . who is I suppose you would have to say incurably . . . And then Robin, my daughter back in Australia, my daughter from my first marriage, Robbie got into trouble in school, well she got herself expelled to tell you the truth, and Faith, my first wife, the one I saw . . . the one I thought I saw today . . . Faith called.''

And Carolyn, his second wife, had thrown a tantrum. "Faith just never gives up, does she?'' she'd stormed.

"But it's Robbie,'' he'd said bewildered, preoccupied with his daughter, furious with her, sick with anxiety.

"Hah!'' Carolyn had shouted. *"Hah!''*

"What do you mean, *hah?''*

"Hah!'' Carolyn screamed. Then she burst into tears. "Can't you *see,''* she demanded, "why she puts Robin up to those things? Can't you *see?''*

He could see that Carolyn's knuckles were white with strain. Sometimes it seemed to him that her body was covered with small sharp spikes.

"It's so obvious,'' Carolyn's voice was climbing higher, higher. "First the broken ribs, then the stealing, and now this . . . this *perversion*. She only puts Robin up to it to get your attention.''

He was frightened for Carolyn sometimes, though Carolyn seemed to glide protected on the slipstream of her own incommensurate furies. She scooped up the twins and swept out of the apartment and slammed the door with such force that his University of Sydney beer mug fell off his desk — a theatrical statement that was rather spoiled for Carolyn by her having to return for the children's snowsuits.

"I could never make head or tail of it,'' Adam sighed. "She just packed up and went home to her mother in Perth. Took the children with her.''

"What did you do?''

"Me? Well, nothing.'' He had been so *relieved*. "Of

course it was distressing but what could I possibly . . .?
I had to finish my year, I was on a Fullbright. And
Rhoda was very helpful —''

"The therapist.''

"Yes. And then my book came out, and Cal State offered me a visiting appointment, and then San Diego,
and then Smith. I never got around to going back.''

Sandra lay watching the ceiling. She composed a letter
to her old roommate: *Oh these predictable Smith pro-
fessors. It's talk, not sex, that turns them on.* Her roommate was backpacking up the Himalayas in quest of
Tantric eroticism and other highs of a spiritual nature.
The love life of male intellectuals, Sandra telegraphed to
her, *continues to be a quest for the perfect listener.
There are times when I believe myself doomed to the
role of intelligent voluptuous ear. But then, in these
days of wine and AIDS, who am I to complain?*

"And Rhoda-the-therapist?'' she prompted, to set
Adam's quest back in motion.

"Well actually, that didn't last very long,'' he said —
for Rhoda, who was and always would be in aggressive
good health, world without end, amen, Rhoda believed
they should all be *friends*, he and she and Faith and
Carolyn and all the children and God knew who else.
She tried to get him, for example, to telephone his wives
on their birthdays. Of course he would not. If you
reopen Pandora's box, you deserve what you get. "So
she wrote letters,'' he groaned, "to Faith and Carolyn.
She actually wrote letters to them.'' Of course, neither
Faith nor Carolyn ever replied.

"Rhoda's so American. She never understood about
Australian women.'' Nor about Australian men. For
Rhoda still sent him care packages and birthday wines
and invitations to dinner parties that she and her new
husband were hosting. She never gave him a moment to

mourn for her, the way he did for his first two wives.

For sorrow, that sweet poetic enduring emotion, Rhoda had not the slightest knack.

He frowned, and stared at the night table beside the bed. "I keep thinking I hear a phone ringing," he said. "I keep thinking I hear the long-distance pips."

In Sydney, Robin pictures Northampton, Massachusetts, and the small postcard-pretty faculty house with sash windows that stick. She pictures the ill-fitting storm frames that let in the draught. She and Natalie visited last year, a mistake. She pictures the phone in the empty living room. She pictures the hundred-year-old windows rattling softly as the phone rings and rings and rings.

"Ten," Robin counts. "Eleven. Twelve rings. The bastard. Always unreachable when needed, how does he do it?"

"Why don't you hang up?" Natalie asks. "What's the point of letting it go on ringing?"

"Cheap satisfaction," Robin smiles. "Thirteen. Fourteen. I like to think of it jarring his house, and it's free." She looks out the window, past several tacky high rises, toward the strip of Cronulla beach. Some things replay themselves, though she lives resolutely in the present. Still, from the look of her shirred bathing suit, yes she must be nine or ten years old. Eighteen years ago if you keep that kind of score.

"It's still yesterday there, right?" Natalie says. "It's still yesterday afternoon. He's probably at his office."

Robin cradles the receiver against her neck and hoists herself onto the windowsill. It's hot outside, a steamy January day. "Snowing where you are?" she asks the house in Northampton. She can see unemployed Sydney teenagers cruising the beachfront in battered cars, looking for a safe spot to dope up. She can see mothers assembling clusters of children with buckets and spades, rubber floats, towels tied around their necks like Superman capes. She sees her mother a little apart from the other mums, never quite one of the group. Her father is still inside the rented holiday flat, possibly reading a book, possibly following the footie. ("Aussie Rules is football for intellectuals," he says.) He is cavalier about when he joins them on the beach. Sometimes when she is just getting ready for bed he insists that they all go for a moonlight romp in the waves. Sometimes at low tide he announces "Footie time!" and practises his drop kicks on the hard wet sand and makes Robin chase the football and bring it back.

Today he is staying inside the flat.

Robin and her mother spread their towels on the sand, and Faith rubs suntan oil on the child's shoulders and back. They spread white zinc ointment on each other's noses, and make white clown lips, and wrinkle up their faces and laugh, though it seems to Robin that there is always something small and sad, like a ship's bell in fog, deep down in the well of her mother's laughter. Robin looks down the golden slope toward the ocean and jiggles from one foot to the other with impatience; her mother is kneeling, the tube of zinc ointment in her hands, facing back toward the houses.

A change happens. First it touches Faith's hands which tremble for an instant and then turn softer and gentler on Robin's skin. Robin watches the change move across her mother the way a wave moves up the sand. It spreads a *shining*. And the child laughs with sheer happiness because a weight has been taken off her chest. "Oh Mummy!" she says, locking her arms around Faith's neck, happy, happy.

The mother strokes the child's hair and nuzzles the crook of her neck and looks at the houses. The child turns. Her father is crossing the road, waving, jogging toward them. Against her cheek the child feels the breath of her mother, how it has turned fast and sweet. It reminds the child of something, it smells like . . . like . . .? like grass after mowing; like the moment when her father puts the mower in the shed and flops down in the shade and reaches up to take the beer from her mother's hand. Her father, zigzagging between traffic, waves and calls out. He flashes his white teeth at them.

The sun is up, everything is different. But then . . .

But then a stray football passes through the air between them and without a thought her father leaps and catches. It is beautiful, Robin thinks, the way he moves. There are shrieks. Giggles. A knot of teenage girls, brown thighs flashing, jumps, laughs, entices, moves in a million directions, clutching for the football, waiting for his pass. He runs, he is engulfed, he makes his pass. And Robin can feel how cold it is on the towels where a shadow has fallen.

Faith looks away, tents a hand over her eyes and scans the empty Pacific. She holds herself very still. She smiles very brightly. "Go and swim, darling," she says, with only the slightest tremor in her voice. "I'll join you in a minute."

Robin puts her head down and runs straight for the core of the football melee. "Daddy, Daddy!" she calls, and yes somewhere in all those limbs she finds his hand, she extracts him, she tacks up the beach with him.

"Come on then," he laughs, and the three of them run down the beach and into the surf. The three of them. Robin is in the middle, her mother on one side, her father on the other.

"Bastard," she murmurs, letting the phone rattle his windows in Northampton, Massachusetts. She hangs up and buries her face in her hands. "Bastard!" she calls out the window. Natalie goes to her, holds her. "Daddy!" Robin sobs. "Daddy, *please.*" She cannot stop sobbing.

In his haste, Adam fumbles the keys and drops them in snow. He can hear the phone ringing inside. Damn. He brushes at several inches of white powder on his doorstep. Damn. Where the bloody hell are the keys?

The phone stops ringing.

He gropes around in the dark with a gloved hand, hears the clink of metal, closes his clumsy fingers around the keys, lets himself in. The house is deafeningly horribly quiet. Against the great sludge of silence he pushes his shoulder and stumbles into his kitchen. He feels ill with anxiety. Lights, music, *the king rises!* Lights, lights, lights!

He turns on the television. "You cannot *create* faith," a midnight preacher says earnestly. His certainties coat him like a slick of suntan oil. *Cronulla*, Adam thinks for no reason. The word falls out of nowhere, a black spider of sound, a little leggy knob at the end of a swaying thought. "Faith is a gift," the TV evangelist says. "It is a letting go."

"Oh shut up!" Adam snarls and snaps off the set. Pouring Scotch, his hands shake so much that an amber spill licks at his table like a wave on a Sydney beach. He holds the glass up to the light. "I made the TV say those words," he tells it. "I put those words in the box. Bloody amazing what the mind will do. A bloody amazing machine." He drinks the Scotch neat. "I'm spooked," he tells the carpet, pouring himself another drink.

"What time is it there now?" Natalie asks.

"Middle of the night," Robin says. "There's no point trying again. He must be away."

"Maybe you should call Carolyn. Doesn't she always keep tabs on exactly where he is because of the child support?"

"I'd rather die," Robin says. "She'd accuse Mum of staging her death to get attention."

Natalie says nothing.

"I'll try one more time," Robin says. "For the heck of it."

"Robin!" Adam lurches into the night table. "My god, *Robbie!*" Something shifts inside his body. *Yes,* his body says, *this is it.* This is what we have been dreading. The phone clatters to the floor, the knocked-over bottle of Scotch glugs all over it.

"Oh Daddy," she says. She cannot speak.

Robbie? he asks, tries to ask, but no sound will come to his aid. In any case, to what point? Because he knows, he knows. "Robbie," he whispers gruffly. He could be spitting his way through gravel. "I saw her. I saw her yesterday in New York. She looked so beautiful, Robbie. I did love her, you know."

Yes, he realises now, he did. He does. *He does.* Something tears away from inside him. A miscarriage, he thinks in vague pain. A hysterectomy. He could be bleeding, he could be wetting himself.

"Oh Daddy," Robin sobs. "Right to the end, she believed you'd visit before she — She kept on making allowances."

There's so much white noise, it roars in his ears.

"Robbie," he asks. "What's that smell? I smell —" he sniffs; a bubble of something, of anguish, of laughter, gurgles up — "I smell salt, I smell surf."

"It's the beach," Robin says. "We're in a flat at Cronulla."

We. Robbie and. . . . He feels the mule kick of anger and revulsion but bites his lip hard.

"I'll get a flight tomorrow, Robbie," he says.

He finishes the bottle of Scotch and falls asleep on his living-room carpet. He dreams.

On the hard sand, the wet sand, the line of foam licks around his ankles. His back is wonderfully arched, he's on the World's Most Sensuous deckchair, the Great Australian Bight, the famous Bighter, he is cradled by the map of Australia. Silly blighter, Australia teases. Her Queensland finger tickles him, Victoria cushions his head, a wave catches him by the Perthy regions and he floats eastward into the Pacific. This is warm, this is womb fluid, Robin is just being born, not a thing has gone wrong yet, time itself is barely beginning.

Amazing visions come and go in the glass-green walls of the waves, the white crests are creamed with prophecy, a row of little fishes pauses and stares, and Faith, Faith with her sweet bride's face, is coming at him with the speed of light. Effortlessly he turns, he reaches, a perfect catch. It's a gift, it's a gift, laughs Robin, capering on the golden sands of Cronulla.

Now I Lay Me Down to Sleep

I'm particular about the time I go. It's a private thing, I don't want people staring. Best of all are these long summer evenings when the light hangs on, mauve and coy, in a way that makes me think of Mary Pickford. You remember how she took forever to leave the screen? — a trace of perfume, a trace of sadness, a long slow fadeout. America's Sweetheart, I've cried for her hundreds of times on the late late reruns, I've lived all her lives. It's one of her films — I forget which one — that I think of when I climb through the chain-link gap behind the privet. (The wrought-iron gates have already been locked when I visit.) In my mind I'm always wearing trailing silk, cream-coloured, with little seed pearls along the hemline.

So I am dressed to go — I have added, in my mind, a bonnet with lace veil, a parasol, gloves, the trappings of tragic occasion — when my brother Kevin arrives. I know it's Kevin from the sound of his front bumper. He parks imprecisely. I hear him stumble past the first landing and call a noisy greeting at the turn in the stairs. "Kevin?" quavers Mrs O'Sullivan who lives on the ground floor, who's been our tenant for centuries. But he stumbles on. He raps loudly on my door, but doesn't wait for me to open it.

"Monica!" He smothers me in a hug.

"Oh Kevin, I was just going out."

"Tha's wunnerful, Mon. I'll go wisher . . . I'll go'sh . . ." He sucks in his cheeks and pinches his lips to show contempt for these words falling out like junk from an overstuffed closet. He rummages, pulls at syllables one by one, extracts them carefully, triumphantly: "I'll . . . go . . . with . . . you."

"Oh Kevin. I can't believe you *drove*."

"Hey!" he says, unjustly accused. "Hey! S'jus the mouth. Perfeckly orright 'cept for lips. 'N maybe tongue." He balances delicately, first on one leg and then the other, to show that he has absolute control of the larger muscles. He twists his arms into a pretzel and winks at me through his fingers. He shadow-boxes, does a little dance shuffle. "C'mon, Mon. Aren't you going to invite me in for dinner?"

"I've eaten already. Anyway," I say, "the football trophies are all at Mrs Quinn's. She took them home to polish them."

"Lemme see." He pushes anxiously past me, down the hall.

"She'll bring them back on Friday."

"S'okay," he says, curling himself up in the old armchair. "S'okay. You mind if I stay for a night or two?"

"Oh Kevin," I sigh. "Is it Margaret?"

"S'nothing. S'nothing. Doncha like having me? Wher' you going?"

"Just for a walk. You haven't been laid off again?"

"I told you, s'nothing. Where we going?"

"Nowhere. Just walking. You can watch TV."

"I'm coming."

"No, Kevin, I don't want . . ."

"Monica," he says heavily, protectively. "Allow me." He offers his arm, makes an elaborate bow, trips.

So what can I do? I'll have to give up this evening's visit, forget the gap behind the privet. I don't want to tell anyone yet. Sometimes, when I look at Kevin, I think: he'll go the way dad did. There are rules for families like ours, Boston Irish, we can't break them. God gets one son (that's Patrick, Father Pat, he'll bury us) and one goes to the devil. The daughters marry and produce Catholic broods, except for one — the eldest (that's me), or the youngest, or maybe just the plainest. She's needed home to look after Ma and Pa till they go, then to pick up the family pieces.

"Where we going, Mon?"

"Nowhere. Just walking." Up Common to Trapelo Road, down the long hill, turn right, along past the wrought-iron gates (don't look), on into the park.

"Wassermatter with your hands?"

Without thinking, I say: "I'm unbuttoning my gloves."

"Wha . . .?" He stops and stares down at me, frowning. "What gloves? Whad'ya talking about?" He puts his hands on my shoulders. Even whisky-softened, they are the hands of an old football star, of a construction worker. "Mon? You okay?"

Good, I think. He's sobering up. I keep walking. I *am* okay, as long as I can handle it my own way.

"What d'ya mean . . . *gloves*?" he persists.

No gloves, no parasol, this isn't the same walk. "Nothing," I say. "Ask a silly question."

Not that Mary Pickford would have chosen Belmont. More like Cambridge, more like Mt Auburn Cemetery with its view of the Boston skyline across the Charles: better headstones, more trees, a view of the Harvard and MIT racing eights on the river. More famous company. I won't pretend that I don't get wistful. But I think there's a rule, I think you have to have proof of residence, I think it's got something to do with city taxes. Anyway, it's not the sort of thing you want to go asking questions about. You can't just call up City Hall and ask if you're eligible for Cambridge. Not with dignity.

"Monica," my mother used to say, "don't get ideas. A girl should know her place." She was never wrong about anything, she would have been the first to admit it. When Kevin used to yell at her — he was her favourite, the one who got her maddest — when he used to storm out and slam the door, she would press her lips together and put her hand over her heart. Then she would say (not to me, exactly, more to the peas she was shelling or the pastry she was rolling or to the Blessed Virgin in her gilt frame over the refrigerator): "I may not know very much, but I know when I'm right."

Even Kevin admitted it. "What I can't stand, Mon," he said to me once, before she died, in his wandering whisky voice, "is the way she's so goddamn right about everything. Jesus! How do you stand it?"

"Well," I sighed, "she was right about Dennis Bouchard, so what can I do?"

"Oh Mon. Poor Mon. Have a drink." It was Crown Whiskey, his hip-flask standby. For a royal pain, he said. And I did — just a few sips — because I was thinking about the first and last time I brought Dennis Bouchard home. And afterwards Ma sniffing: "You're getting ideas, my girl. If you think for one minute that a man who looks like that one is ever going to —"

"Ma," I said, "he's got a little boy. He's a widower." (It was a miracle, of course, a miracle. I knew it was too good to be true.) "He's got a house on Beacon Hill," I said. "Right near the Common."

"Beacon Hill!" she laughed. She couldn't see me on Beacon Hill.

And as always, she was right, so horribly right that I had to hide the *Globe* and the *Herald* for days. I couldn't bear to have her purse her lips and raise her eyes to the Blessed Virgin or the Sacred Heart.

"Kevin," I say, back in the present. "Who got Ma's Sacred Heart?"

"Ginny got it. Keeps it on the pantry door."

"This is a dreadful thing to say, but it used to make me think of raw liver."

Kevin laughs, but then quickly crosses himself, and does some soft-shoe on the sidewalk. Suddenly I see him as an altar boy again, lace ruffs and freckles and missing tooth and grubby sneakers under the smock. Everybody's golden boy. I'm sorry I mentioned raw liver. These days I'm not so quick to think thoughts like that. These days, sometimes, I wouldn't mind the Sacred Heart on my dresser.

"Mon, why're you crying?"

"I'm not crying." I look back to adjust my silk train. The little seed pearls are snagging on the past, there are details clinging like burrs. The taste of Dennis Bouchard's lips, for example. The way his hair came to a soft point at the nape. The reasons why so many women — as it turned out — agreed to marry him and look after his little boy. "I was thinking of Dennis Bouchard."

"Jesus," Kevin says. He swings himself around a tree, once, twice, like a top. "Jesus," he says again. "When we mess up, Mon!"

But I have the parasol back now, and the button gloves, Mary Pickford's gloves.

It's your eyes, Dennis Bouchard said, the day we met. This was in the rectory, after a funeral, when I was secretary for Father Molloy. I twirl my parasol over my shoulder. I remember how I wanted to tell Father

Molloy: You've never admitted the truth about mortal
sin, you've never said how delicious, how it makes you
feel that eternal damnation doesn't *matter* . . . But I
never said that to him, not even in confession.

Down through my spinning parasol, here it comes:
the first time Dennis drove me out to Walden Pond.
Late October, no crowds, and we sat in the car and he
stroked my breasts and sucked the nipples like a baby.

I feel weak inside and have to lean against a tree, I ar-
range my train, I draw circles in the grass with the point
of my parasol. We are standing in the park, Kevin is
watching the kids play baseball with their dads.

"Why don't you bring J.J.?" I ask him.

Wrong question. I can see his heart jump like a fish.
There might as well be a window in his chest, I can see it
turn, I can see it jounce like raw liver.

"Jeez, Mon," he says, turning away.

The Donnellys cry easily, they wear their hearts on
their sleeves, you can buy them in cheap gilt frames.

"Oh Kevvy. Next weekend then. We'll play baseball,
we'll drive out to the Arboretum."

"It's *this* weekend," he says. "This is *my* weekend.
She's taken him to the Cape with that jerk, that filthy-
rich . . ." He is hurling stones into a clump of forsythia.
A word travels with each missile, is rung up against the
chain link behind the bushes: "Smart . . . ass . . .
prick . . ."

"I knew this had something to do with Margaret," I
begin, as the wordstones clatter and someone's dad
yells: "Hey, you! Don't you know there are little
kids . . .?" and Kevin rams his hands into his pockets
and begins walking in a race to nowhere.

"Got a cabin there, the jerk!" he says when I catch
up, though he doesn't slow down, he is late for
something. *"Mister* Respectable!"

I'm stumbling, I've had to abandon my train. "Kevin, Kevin," I gasp. Sudden exertion is where I notice the deterioration most. "Kevin, I have to . . . I think I'm going to . . ." It seems to come at me from the ankles up, like water rising. Suddenly nothing is solid below the neck and I am dissolving right here at the border of the park where it meets the street.

"Mon!" Kevin yells. "Holy Mother, what the —?" He arranges me on a park bench, my flounces and seed pearls horribly askew. "Oh Jeez," he says. "I forgot."

"Summer 'flu." I'm breathing slowly, moving my thoughts around the edges of the pain. Soon I won't be able to climb over it. "It's nothing. Getting old, I guess.. Can't hurry the way I . . ."

"Mon!" He has his hands on my shoulders, he is trying to look me in the eye but I'm studying the Little Leaguers. "Mon, do you think we don't know? You're skinny as a whippet, for God's sake. You weigh like nothing. Anyway, Dr Wright told Pat and Father Pat told Ginny and Ginny told me."

Busybodies. It's not their place.

"We know and we don't know," Kevin says, tapping his forehead, puzzled. "It's hard to . . . I guess I hoped it was all a . . . Jeez, you look dreadful, Mon."

"It's okay," I say. "It comes and goes. It's no big deal."

"You got to quit work."

"I know. Soon. I'm going to ask for leave of absence."

"Leave of absence!"

"Extended."

"Extended!" He pounds his fist into the park bench. "Oh Jeez, Mon!"

"Hey!" I say. "It's no big deal. Listen, I'm going to show you something. I'll need to lean on your arm."

So we walk along the edge of the park, back toward Belmont Street, and turn left into Fairweather, and I show him the hole in the chain link, behind the privet. "Jeez, Mon," he says. "Do we have to?"

"I'd like to, Kev."

"Jeez," he says, pulling the hip-flask out. "I could do with a drink."

But he follows me between the stone markers, the *Here lieth*s . . . and the *Beloved wife of*s . . . up the hill, down a little valley, to my spot. There's an elm tree — it must be just about the only one left in all of Massachusetts — hanging over it, and a bunch of lilacs to the side. I lie down on the grass, all cream silk and seed pearls and flounces. "I tried them all," I say, "and this is the spot I picked. It's all paid up. Look, you can't see the highrises from here. Just elm tree and clouds."

"Oh, Jeez," he says, rubbing his sleeve across his eyes. "Oh Jeez, Mon. When we mess up!"

"Come here." I pat the grass beside me. "And stop crying. Listen, I'm going to tell you what I'd like. It's something I haven't even told Father Pat yet. See the lilacs? That's where you and J.J. should stand, right under the elm. Margaret doesn't even have to come. We won't invite her."

He winces and hugs himself. There's a small moaning sound.

"Are you going to tell me why you came to visit this evening?" I ask.

"She's getting an annulment."

"Oh Kevin."

"She'll get custody, she always gets what she wants."

"Look at that cloud," I say. "With the hook on it. Ma wagging her finger and saying we'd come to no good."

We both stare up through the elm.

"No," he says. "It's Margaret's claws." He laughs harshly. "It's a crooked mile." He laughs again and tosses pebbles up at the sky. "Mon?"

"Hmm?"

"You and Dennis Bouchard, before they caught him . . . Did you ever, you know . . .?"

"Yes," I say. "We did. But if you're worried that I'm in a state of mortal sin . . ."

"I'm glad," he says sombrely. "Nobody should have to, you know . . . I mean, even though everyone messes it up. Still. Anyway, I'm glad." He rolls over onto his stomach in the grass. "Son of a gun!" he says. "That Dennis . . .!" He begins to laugh. "In spite of everything, in spite of Ma."

"Well," I say modestly. "Ma didn't realise."

"Ma didn't . . .!" He splutters, rolling in the grass, and we laugh and laugh and laugh.

Queen of Pentacles,
Nine of Swords

First I noticed her condition, then her startling nose-jewel (a diamond teardrop), and only after that her remarkable face. This was years ago, the first time she came into my ratty apartment on Earl Street. She was eight months pregnant and nineteen years old at the time, and still wearing *salwar-chemeez;* but the pantaloons were giving her trouble in the snow and she had tucked them into boots that a local pig farmer must have given to the Sally Ann. A vinyl stamp on the uppers said: *Thurston Farms, Kingston, Ont.* The parka was another cast-off, bilious green, its hood ringed with mangy fake fur. Inside it, she had the eyes of a tiger.

On the sofa that served as my waiting room she sat next to a housewife who edged discreetly away. My customers were uneasy with foreigners. They stared. The girl opened her bag (a drawstring sack, beaded and brocaded with elephants and little mirrors) and began to work: fingers flying, a cream silk streamer of crochet snaking out of her hands, twitching, growing, curling under the sofa like some live nervy creature.

Perhaps it was simply that we didn't know Indian women crocheted. I suppose we thought of it as something our grandmothers once did, as something that went out with lavender pomanders and maiden aunts.

(Months later she was to tell me sardonically that ever since 1851, ever since the Great Exhibition and the Crystal Palace, when all the prizes for crochet went to the corners of the empire, it has been Kenyans, Trinidadians, Tamils — whomever the missionaries taught — who have been keeping the lace-making arts alive.)

But back then we knew nothing of that. We stared.

She ignored us, and crocheted as if she were under a curse.

That was seventeen years ago, but it is the first image that comes back to me when Decker calls.

"Metro Toronto Police," he says. "I'm calling in connection with a woman named Sita Ramshankar."

"Oh," I say faintly, bracing myself.

"I know it's a long way, but we'd appreciate it if you could come on into the city, ma'am. Bloor Street station."

"Right now?"

"We'd appreciate it."

In the car, disoriented, I half turn around to see if the boys are safely strapped into the back seat — Sita's son and my son, our little boys who have part-time jobs and are almost through high school now.

I try to remember why the children are not in the car. I stare vaguely at the bunch of keys in my hand and just sit there in my garage.

She is still and always coming into my room with her swollen belly and the diamond blister in her nostril. Something powerful, some strong animal sense, warns me: Don't read her cards. But I am cornered, when it's her turn, by the way she holds out the five-dollar bill and by her eyes. Or perhaps it has something to do with the ribbon of crochet that twitches as she loops it up and stuffs it into her bag. She's the last for the day; there are just the two of us.

"I have seen your advertisement," she says, and the English is sterling, crisp as a new pound note, discordant. She smells of poverty in spite of the diamond teardrop, and her eyes unnerve me.

Listen, I want to say, I don't read for True Believers. I put on this gypsy smock and my dangling earrings (the crescent moon on my left ear, the star on my right), and presto: desolate suburban wives are able to unburden themselves. In the cards they see little Markey who is having trouble at school, and Darlene, who is nubile and recently divorced and always borrowing someone's husband on account of engine trouble, and Mr Dunlap the electrician who didn't install the baseboard heater properly but won't come back to fix it. I promise a letter from Winnipeg, an unexpected visitor from Montreal. I throw in a bit of solemnity, a little closing of the eyes and deep breathing, a pinch of hope, and they go away happy. The housewife's therapist. I'm cheaper, after all, than a night of bingo or a Sears catalogue binge.

I ignore her five dollars and pour her a cup of tea. "What's your name?"

"Sita." She points to the Tarot pack, implying urgency. Between her palms, the money is rolled back and forth, back and forth; it furls itself tighter, becomes a reefer, a taper, a skewer. She looks at it, puzzled, then places it delicately on my saucer.

There are some people . . . I don't know what it is . . . they give off the same kind of hum as high tension cables. You know from the start that if you get too close you'll be singed. And yet they're the very ones — don't you find this? — who make you understand the moths.

Still, I make an effort to resist.

"I can't take your money," I tell her. "Listen, your husband is a graduate student, right? So is mine. This is how I manage, that's all." I show her the crib in the other room, my baby asleep. "This pays a few bills," I say. "But I can't read your cards, I'm a fraud."

For a moment she stares at me, eyebrows raised, then she laughs — a short harsh incredulous sound. "It's the *cards*," she says, as if to the village idiot. "The cards themselves. Don't you understand?" Under her breath she murmurs "Canadians!" and shakes her head. Without asking, she picks up the deck and begins to shuffle. She shuffles vertically, cards fluttering between her hands, descending, then rising mysteriously like geese in formation. "Read," she says, placing the pack in front of me. And as an afterthought: "Please."

She's intense as a junkie, desperate; but also used to power and accustomed to giving orders. Nothing fits. Stalling, I ask: "How long have you been in Canada?"

Eye to eye over the cards, we breathe each other's breath, I can smell coriander and something else, something musky and irresistible and dangerous.

"I have been here six months. There was the marriage, and then I came. It was arranged." She taps the Tarot impatiently. "You are reading the cards now, isn't it?"

There's a certain peremptory tone I've never cared for. "Read them yourself," I say evenly. "I'm not your servant."

Her knuckles turn white and crack like tiny silver pistols. "Please." The fingers are rigid now — the strain of politeness, of supplication. "The importance is very great."

I don't understand why I do it. I cut three times to the left and draw ten cards.

"Ah," I say flippantly, relieved. "Here, in your current situation, we have the Page of Cups, which means the birth of a child is imminent. And he's crossed by the Knight of Cups, who is your husband. But who's this in your past, in the Seven of Swords? This trickster making off with stolen goods?"

She is holding her head in her hands like the ravaged woman in the Nine of Swords who dominates the spread. "Again," she says. "Again, again, again." As though she can feel the prick of the nine deadly swords poised above her.

When was the next time?

Quattrochi's, just a week or so later. Quattrochi's, which is such an unlikely store to find in a small Ontario town, that I've always half suspected it vanishes when I'm not shopping there to believe in it. Quattrochi's smells of cinnamon and saffron; loops of chili peppers, squash flowers, the mysterious ingredients of *garam masala,* all hang from the walls; there are baskets of mangoes, passionfruit, papayas, guavas. I was not surprised, somehow, to see Sita there.

She was stroking the purple bellies of eggplants, prodding their curves with a finger. On the basket, a crayonned sign said: *Spoiled vegetables. Prices reduced.*

"Any day now, I expect," I greeted her politely, leaning across melons and pineapples.

"No," she said, feeling and poking. "It is too late, but they will have to do."

"I meant your baby."

Her eyes widened, then she flashed me that withering look: of scorn? of disbelief? "But I will lose the baby," she said.

I suppose she found me slow, or perhaps wilfully

obtuse. The need to explain exasperated her. *("Cana-dians!")*

"The Nine of Swords." Her fingers drummed on the handle of the shopping cart. "India, England, Canada, it makes no difference."

I blinked. "You're not suggesting . . .?"

"For me, the predictions are always very bad."

"You're just nervous," I assure her, patting her hand. "I was too, this close. It's normal."

"You know nothing." She pinched the skin of an egg-plant savagely, and amethyst rind came away in her hand. "My father got a second opinion. An astrologer was brought from Madras. It was the same."

"I can't believe . . . I mean, you're educated, you're married to a . . ."

"Oh yes, I know," she snapped. "I'm *Canadian* now. The cautious people, the safe people."

"There's no need to be —"

"I will show you. You will read for me again."

"I most certainly will not."

And when I did, back in my Earl Street apartment, it was there again: the Nine of Swords. "You cheated," I accused. "It was the way you shuffled."

She ignored me.

Without, I think, being aware of what she was doing, she fiddled in her drawstring bag and pulled out the ivory hook and began to crochet. Faster, faster, the silken thread creamy and skittish. She never took her eyes off the cards. "Look: the Queen of Staves. She's the headmistress at Finchley Academy for Girls."

"Finchley?"

"In England. I hated England. She shipped me straight back to Tanjore after Mr Timkins . . . He was the history master . . ." She patted her stomach, to in-dicate the nature of homework for Mr Timkins, who would have been helpless, I imagine, from the moment she tossed her black mane and fluttered her slow heavy lashes. I remember feeling a spasm of sympathy for him, fellow fly in a web.

"What happened to Mr Timkins?"

She paused momentarily, puckered her brows, shrugged. "He was fired, I think."

She might have been discussing Mr Dunlap of unsatisfactory electrical installations, or wanton Darlene. "Anyway, Daddy flew to Bombay to meet me. He didn't want me seen in Tanjore. Poor Daddy. But he couldn't say he wasn't warned." The family astrologer had told them over and over: nothing could be done to offset such an inauspicious time of birth.

The snake of crochet jumped and twitched and lay still.

"So what else could Daddy do? In Canada, Daddy said, they don't even have shame." Add to Canada — *Canada!* — a student husband, a family with no money: it was what they could salvage, she said. She was married by proxy. Her husband met her in Montreal. She said wistfully: "My sister lives in Paris. She is married to an executive of Burma Shell."

"I imagine Daddy will take care of everything," I said tartly. "Here's the Queen of Pentacles. You're going to be rich and famous."

"Rich." Her lip curled. "My family has great wealth." She made a gesture with her fingers, as of flicking away a dandelion puffball, to show how much great wealth meant. "I'm off Daddy's hands now. I'm Ramshankar's problem. I'll lose the baby," she said.

She did lose the baby, but then there was another, her husband's this time. And then another.

Here's a fresh picture, fallen suddenly into focus:

We are sifting through a table of children's snowsuits at the Salvation Army Thrift Store. Sita is feeling the padding of a powder blue suit, assessing the thin spots. She tugs at the jammed zipper, which comes away in her hands like a tear along a dotted line.

"You can stitch it," I say.

She says: "Ramshankar is leaving me."

"What?"

"He is suing for custody of the children."

"What?"

"On account of my affair."

I stare at her, dumbfounded.

"You know Professor Parkinson?" she asks.

"In the Business School?"

"That one. It's him."

I smooth out the tattered lining of a snowsuit that is covered with blips of mildew, and with larger black blotches. Car grease, perhaps. The table stinks of recycled odours. A *lover*, I think. I see bodies gliding and writhing like swans in the quilted tangle of hollow arms and legs. I push my hand down the inside of a sleeve and think hungrily: *another man's skin*. "I had no idea," I mumble. "I've never seen you with —"

"Oh, *seen!* I'm not for being seen with. I'm for hot fucking and sly bragging."

"Well," I say, nervously. "The mother always gets the children."

"Ramshankar knows how to do these things, from Law School. It's interesting, what stirs a man to life." She is racing the broken zipper head up and down its aimless track, up and down. "Ramshankar is so . . . you wouldn't believe how *poor!* I don't mean money; it has nothing to do with money. But he is a *poor* man, a *poor* man." She is spitting the words.

"There is no spirit, there is nothing." She pays for the blue snowsuit with her Family Allowance cheque. Her hand is trembling slightly as she signs her name. "Anyway, before I became a little too hot for comfort, Parkie had me write that Admissions thing." She laughs, and says sardonically: "Apparently I'm brilliant." She makes a mistake with her address on the back of the cheque and has to initial it. "It will be simpler without the children for a few years, actually. I'm starting a business degree."

In the car, we strap the toddlers into their safety seats. "Anyway," she begins, but suddenly buries her face in the zipperless blue snowsuit and holds it there all the way to the Co-op Nursery School. The boys — my Joey and her Ravi — come running to the car with their play-dough airplanes and fingerpainted pictures of happy families. "Anyway, if I'm destitute, I can always sell crochet. You wouldn't believe what the Yorkville boutiques are beginning to pay for that stuff."

This strikes her as funny. She begins to laugh and can't seem to stop. She scoops up her son and tries to stifle her hilarity by nuzzling the hollow of his neck. She stuffs one of his mismatched mittens into her mouth. Whoops of laughter escape like bubbles under pressure.

Her son looks frightened.

We're in a restaurant in this scene, we're in Toronto in a restaurant off Bay Street. The wine steward is tripping over his own feet with obsequious nervousness in Sita's presence. She orders a bottle of something French, the price of which makes me gulp once or twice, and brushes him away.

"So." She picks at her smoked salmon with a fork, nibbles a flowerlet of parsley. "What do you hear from Joey about Ravi?"

"Well, you know," I say nervously. "Grade 12 and Grade 10, they're different countries. It's only during basketball season . . ." I feel ill at ease for being so ordinary: still living in a small town, still married, still on speaking — even on hugging — terms with my children.

"A place like that," she says. "People talk all the time. Everyone knows everyone's business."

"But I never pay attention . . . You know I can't stand that sort of . . ." I have no intention of telling her the rumours. What can you expect, people say, of a kid with a mother who . . .? It's a town that disapproves of the unusual. (There are people who claim to have seen Sita on lower Yonge Street. Late at night, they say, walking up and down and wearing skin-tight leather pants. People will say anything.) Ravi, in fact, is often at our house since his father joined a law firm in Calgary. Ravi sort of camps around. But there's too much in the past for me to tell her any of this. There's the business of the kidnapping, for example, and of Ravi and Prem running away again to their father — or perhaps simply back to the known circle of school friends. Anyway, just too much past. "Ravi's okay," I say. "He's an okay kid. He's an *interesting* kid, Sita. Give him time, he'll come to cherish the fact he has an extraordinary mother."

With her fork, she has divided the smoked salmon into multiple thin strips, none of which she has eaten. "Prem writes," she says. "He has to do it secretly. He has to sneak out to the Calgary post office. He wants me to get him away from his father."

With great concentration, I break a dinner roll apart and butter it.

"I had a reading done last month," she says. "Some U of T student wife. Guess what card came up?"

"Queen of Pentacles, I imagine. I can't believe you

still go in for that stuff.''

"Queen of Pentacles, too, for what that's worth.''

"Worth plenty, apparently. Remember I predicted fame and fortune way back? How does it feel to be made a partner?''

"To be the token woman and token black in the company, you mean? I drive them crazy. They can't stand it that I crochet in board meetings.''

I try to imagine this. I see a circle of pinstriped men, a flash of smoke and vermilion sparks, a little dervish of crochet twisting and turning on the boardroom table. Sita plays on her snake-charmer's pipes. There is a drowsy smell of incense and the men with silver hair and combed moustaches begin to sway and rise like cobras with the wisp of crochet. Sita keeps time with her ivory needle, hooking, hooking.

"I'm bored out of my mind in strategy meetings,'' she says vehemently. "All these people who can only do one thing at a time. I have to listen to their minds crawling along, clunk, clunk, clunk. I'm going to have to move on, find something with more bite to it. Do you ever get the feeling when you wake in the morning that you just want to sink your teeth into the day, and suck at it and suck at it? And it never *ever* has enough juice to make it worthwhile?''

"Sita, you can't just . . . Can't you see that you're *programming* yourself for . . . I mean, this obsession with the Nine of Swords. And inauspicious birth, for God's sake! You've got a terribly self-destructive —''

"Ah,'' she says cuttingly. "Psychology. The Canadian form of the occult.''

"You worry me. You haven't eaten a thing.''

"I'm ravenous. *Ravenous!*'' she says.

*   *   *

Sergeant Decker is ill at ease. "I can't figure this lady. I just can't figure her. Appreciate your coming all this way." He goes to a file cabinet, rifles through a drawer, pulls out a blue manila folder. "Long drive. How was the 401?"

"Uh . . . so-so." But I cannot remember what the traffic was like. I cannot remember getting here at all.

He is shaking his head. "Third time in as many months. Little twist to this one, though. This time she's not at the receiving end. No smashed-up lip, no bruises." His eyebrows lift. "You didn't know about that?"

For some reason, I notice there is a slat missing in the Venetian blind on the window above his desk. Third from the top.

"She gave you as next-of-kin. She — ah — married to a relative or something? Well, none of my business." He looks through the folder. "Yeah,'"he says. "Yeah. She has a taste for violent johns."

Then he settles himself into his chair and leans across his desk. "What really blows our minds," he says, and I note the proprietary cast to his voice. He likes to talk about her. His case. "Turns out she's a big wheel on Bay Street. Well, of course you know. I check it out because of the too fancy car, which I assume is her pimp's and probably stolen. Trail leads to this glitzy building. I step out of the elevator on the sixteenth floor and she's standing there in this grey suit with a red silk thing around her neck. Looking like the ice princess herself. You could've knocked me over with a feather. Course," he says. "Coloureds. You never know, do you?"

He tosses a sheet of paper in front of me. "Arrest, this time. Shoplifting. Has to appear in court on the 14th."

"Now —" He leans forward, resting his chin on his clasped hands. "That lady must make two, three times what I make. Something weird is going on here."

I nod. I feel a little sick. The missing slat in the Venetian blind seems to have ominous importance. I swallow, I mentally rehearse words, I form the question in my mind. But do I want to know? Decker goes on as though I have asked anyway.

"Woolworths. Fifteen, twenty dollars worth of junk. Yarn. Silk thread. The kind of stuff ladies do embroidery with. Crochet hooks. You willing to take her with you?"

I nod.

When she is brought out, I see the way he gets nervous. Oh Decker, I think. You too. He rushes her a little with awkward courtesies: returning her labelled possessions, handing her his pen for the signature. A policewoman takes her into the next room for photographs. Decker shakes his head, fondly possessive. "Just can't figure her," he says. "Crazy Paki."

"Sita," I say in the restaurant across from the police station. "I'm taking you home with me."

"Not there," she says with a shudder. "I couldn't ever go back there. That was the worst place, the worst place of all."

"But Sita, they were good years. Those years when the children were little —"

She looks me directly in the eyes and I feel glib. "You weren't me," she says. She fiddles in her bag and pulls out her ivory hook and a ball of silk. She begins to crochet by instinct, without looking at the work in her hands. "I've got friends who have a cottage north of Barrie," she says. "Tamils. I'll go there for a while. Can you drop me at the Voyageur terminal?''

"No, I'm not going to do that. At least I'll take you home for your car.''

"I can't *stand* the car. It's so . . . nothing *happens* in the car. Will you take me to Dundas Street, or do I have to get a cab?''

At the bus terminal, I catch hold of her arm. "Sita, I'm afraid to leave you.''

For just the merest second, she permits herself to be held. She butts her forehead against mine. "Don't blame yourself,'' she says. "No one could have done anything.'' She clears her throat. "Tell Ravi . . .'' Then she shakes me off. "Listen,'' she says. "I don't want you hanging around.''

But I do hang around. I stand shivering out on Dundas Street, watching through the grimy glass doors of the waiting room, as she sits there crocheting feverishly. I watch right up until a man with a shaved head and a tattoo on his arm saunters over and puts his foot on the chair next to hers. He leans toward her. His boot is close to her thigh. There is something about his swagger that I don't like, I don't like at all. But she smiles up at him and begins to stuff her crochet work into her drawstring bag.

A week later Decker calls.

A Little Night Music

He was an eleventh-hour passenger. Lucy, watching from her window seat, saw the caterpillar-like entrance tunnel begin to draw away from the plane's side, then pause and quiver as though it sensed danger through its furry pleats. In Seat 8A, she was close enough to observe the activity up front, the cockpit door opening and then closing, the steward glued to his transmitter, the mild flurry to unbolt the exit door again. Outside, the caterpillar sniffed at empty space, quested blindly about for a moment, then nosed back toward the aircraft's side. Next thing, the late passenger was stowing a carry-on and a trench coat into the locker above 8B. The carry-on was a maroon sports tote with a white *Esprit* logo on its side.

Damn, Lucy thought, though in spite of herself she felt interest. The late passenger's face was vaguely familiar. An actor? A singer? At any rate, a space invader. It was a night flight, the London-Frankfurt-Singapore leg, and when the door had been sealed earlier she'd realised with relief that she'd be able to push the armrest up, curl her legs onto the second seat, and get some proper sleep. Then Darwin, then Brisbane — the longest way home, but she'd had no choice. And now sitting upright. She beamed her chagrin at the late passenger's profile.

He was very pale, that was the next thing she noticed; pale in spite of dark hair and dark eyes and what presumably should have been olive skin. It was as though he'd been without sun for a long time, been hibernating, living in a basement or something.

"You look familiar," she said. "Aren't you famous?"

He appeared not to hear. Twice, fumbling with the seat belt, he failed to get the buckle to snap shut. He swore softly, not in a language Lucy recognised. His hand shook.

Well, that was understandable. All day long, Lucy (and no doubt the entire world population of airport and transit-lounge sojourners) had been mentally reciting statistics: Safer than driving on an expressway. Safer than writing novels that offend the faithful. Safer than mixing one valium with a double whisky, which she'd done barely an hour earlier in order to get herself onto the plane.

Nothing worked very well. Not even Mozart coming through her headphones could silence the other voice, the rogue channel. *Coincidence, synchronicity, fate,* the rogue channel thrummed. *Why me?* it asked, running heavy interference with *Eine Kleine Nachtmusik.* If the missed connection meant anything at all, the message was surely deliverance. But what future obligations might such deliverance entail?

She offered the late passenger, by way of fellow feeling: "Would you believe I was supposed to be on last night's flight? We had air traffic control foul-ups in Toronto. Got to London six hours late — fuming, naturally — and missed the fateful connection. Gives you a really weird feeling."

He grunted, twisting about awkwardly, and his seat buckle snapped shut at last. But he'd managed to get the belt caught under hers and when he straightened up she felt a jerk like a tourniquet around her stomach. "Ugh!" she gasped, winded, and he started violently. "Hey," — instinctively she put her hand on his — "hey, it's okay. Everyone feels the same. I had to dope myself just to get through the gate." His hand was icy, and lay like inert matter under hers. "Though logically," she babbled on, "I should feel invulnerable, shouldn't I? A charmed life, one of the chosen." She laughed, too brightly. "Hey, you're safe next to me. I'm a lightning rod of miraculous intervention. Airlines alter their schedules and dislocate hundreds of connections on my account."

He swivelled, jerking her belt again, and looked at her, a stare that went on too long. "I'm sorry," he said when she lowered her eyes, and she could not tell if he was apologising for the stare or for something else. His accent was unplaceable.

"That's okay." One little lunatic, two little lunatics, a whole planeful of crazies, she thought. We're all regressing into infant panic and serves us right for half a century of hubris, flapping through clouds as though Icarus had never fallen from the sky. Nevertheless, white knuckle to white knuckle, they survived take-off.

"Drink before dinner, ma'am?" the stewardess asked.

"God, yes." Lucy breathed deeply, more relaxed now, expansive. "A double shot of whisky, please. On the rocks." She couldn't stop herself: "Do you know I was supposed to be on last night's flight?" *(Idiot. Like old women discussing their operations.)*

"Don't talk about it," the stewardess said. "I swapped with someone, it was on my schedule . . . You can't think about stuff like that, you can't afford to. And for you, sir?''

It was as though he had to translate slowly first. Or as though the words came at him from a very great distance, and he had to wait for the sound to settle. It was as though he were a very old man, hard of hearing, slow of speech, yet he must have been around Lucy's age. Late twenties, she figured. He couldn't be more. Had he been scheduled for last night too?

"A whisky, perhaps?" the stewardess coaxed, and he frowned, trying to decode this, then nodded.

But he didn't drink it, Lucy noticed. He accepted the meal tray, but didn't touch his food. Lucy herself, having successfully defied gravity and fate one more time, was ravenous. The late passenger watched her eat. Lucy laughed a little, embarrassed. "My mother used to say: *starve a fever, feed nerves.*"

He went on staring.

"Last night . . ." she ventured. "You too? Were you . . .?" She might have bruised him. He flinched, and then he reached over and put his hand on her forearm. The frayed shirt cuff and the sleeve of his sport jacket pulled back and she saw the livid bracelet scar at his wrist. "My God," she said. "What happened?" His hand was cold as ice. Probably, she thought, the nerves had been severed. And not so long ago.

Whatever it was, he could not speak of it. Not knowing what else to do, she leaned over and kissed him on the cheek. It was the kind of comfort that a mother gives a child who is afraid of the dark, but it seemed to flick a switch. He caught hold of her arm and returned the kiss passionately, his tongue almost choking her, his good hand sliding under her blouse, skin to skin, his fingers kneading her breasts, thumb against nipple. (How cold his hands were!) It must have been the valium, or else the whisky, or else the simple need for primal comfort. Whatever it was, she responded. These things happen, sometimes, between total strangers on long flights. Or in times of fear.

The stewardess came to take their trays and they broke apart.

"I'm sorry," he said.

"That's okay."

It was gone now, that mad moment, and they both felt embarrassed. Lucy hunched up under an 'airline blanket, a pillow propped into the crook of seatback and wall.

"I'm sorry," he said again, wretchedly. He seemed to be in agony. He wanted absolution for something other than the kissing, she thought.

"That's okay." She patted his icy hand. He withdrew it.

Concert above the Clouds circled through Vivaldi and Beethoven and Liszt, and looped back to Mozart. A little night music, a little light music, a little light, such a tiny amount of light and a long long night; her tongue was tying itself in knots and she slid into sleep.

There was a tunnel which she didn't want to enter, but somebody pushed her. It was black as pitch, black as velvet, and she could feel the pleats of its caterpillar side breathing in and out. The floor heaved. Things *touched* her. She wanted to scream. Somebody hummed a little night music in her ear, and she crawled forward on her hands and knees, trying not to sob, trying to keep her eyes on an infinitely distant wavering dot of light. There was a sudden rush of cold air. Incredibly she was there, at the end of the tunnel. Someone waved a hurricane lantern, spelling semaphore warnings. It was the late passenger. "Don't look down," he wrote with his little light music, but she did. Sheer cliffs fell away into terror, there were updrafts of icy air. Giddiness seized her, she swayed, she clutched at the late passenger and screamed.

"I'm sorry," he was murmuring. "I'm sorry." He picked her blanket up off the floor and tucked it around her. His kiss was like the kiss of mist. She slid down his gentleness into sleep again, back into the very same tunnel, the very same clifftop.

She dreamed that he set the hurricane lantern on a rock and took her violently and rammed his mouth against hers. She dreamed that he spelled *Against the wall* with the hurricane lantern, that he wrote in light: *The shock of history*. She dreamed that they fell over the cliff, entangled, and that his voice fell with them like an echo: *I'm sorry, I'm sorry.*

"Relax!" the stewardess said. "Relax. Thought I'd never get you awake. You slept right through Frankfurt." Picking up blanket and pillows, a bringer of order. "We had an hour, but security was so tight they didn't even let transit passengers off the plane. A few disembarkments, that's all." She was pouring orange juice, removing foil from a steaming omelette. "Funny. You *know* lightning never strikes twice and all that. But I felt safe once we'd got beyond Frankfurt." She popped the cork from a mini bottle of champagne. "We're serving bubbly with breakfast to celebrate."

Lucy noticed that 8B was empty. Bathroom? Or one of those who had disembarked?

"Would you like to see *Die Welt?*" the stewardess asked. "It's all over the front page. They know who did it."

By the light of orange juice and champagne, Lucy turned to *Die Welt* and muddled her way through the German. There was a grainy photograph, unclear, one of those prints that newspapers around the world keep using until certain famous faces seem both familiar and strange in the way that distant relatives in family albums are both known and not known. The plastic explosive, Interpol said, had been smuggled on board in an *Esprit* sports bag. And the perpetrator, a veteran of terrorist offensives, was a young man with the kind of tragic family history that never failed to breed bloody politics. In a recent bomb blast in Beirut, he had lost a hand. He had boarded the flight in London and his remains were identified in the charred wreckage. Heathrow has the best security in the world, Mrs Thatcher said, but plastic explosives are inordinately difficult to . . ..

Lucy pushed the call button for the stewardess. "The late passenger," she asked a little frantically. "Did he get off in Frankfurt?"

"The late passenger?"

"You know, the man who was sitting next to me."

The stewardess raised a quizzical eyebrow. "I don't remember anyone sitting next to you," she said. "Would you like more champagne?"

Here and Now

As it happened, Alison was wearing black when the phone call came; black velvet, cut low in front, with a thin silver chain at her throat. Only minutes before, she had been under the shower. Before that, she had been shovelling snow from the driveway. She had got the car out before the surface slicked over again, and before the city ploughs came through to toss a fresh barricade across the top of the drive. She had showered and put on the black dress. Car keys in hand, she was just pulling the front door shut behind her.

Damn, she thought. Will I answer it or not?

Afterwards it seemed to her that she had known from the first microsecond of the first ring. Four o'clock on a winter's Sunday afternoon, Lake Ontario veined with early ice, darkness already closing in: this is when such phone calls come. In Brisbane it was tomorrow already, it was dawn on Monday morning. Such phone calls are made at dawn.

At the Faculty Club, Alison's car slewed a little on the ice, nudged a parked Toyota, hesitated, then slid obediently into the neighbouring space. She sat trembling slightly, her hands on the wheel, the engine still running, and stared through the windshield at the Brisbane River.

Here, on the lip of the campus, a membrane of ice already stretched across the water for as far as she could see. The membrane was thinner than a fingernail, milky white.

(High in the mango tree, hidden from the other children, frightened, she sucks comfort from the milk iceblocks her mother makes.)

"Metro Toronto engineers," the car radio announced, "are mystified by this morning's explosions in the city's sewer system. Throughout the streets in the downtown core, sewer caps have been popping like champagne corks, an extraordinary sight on a quiet Sunday morning in Toronto."

It is still Sunday here, Alison thought. It is not Monday yet.

It is still now, she thinks.

She turns off radio and ignition and gets out of the car, stepping with infinite care so as not to fracture the thin membranes of ice and time. The air, several degrees below zero, turns into crystal splinters in her lashes and nostrils. Something hurts. It is important to breathe very carefully.

Inside the Faculty Club, champagne corks are popping like pistol shots; a Christmas party, a retirement celebration for a distinguished colleague, two sabbatical farewells, all rolled into one elegant festive affair. Soon Alison will play her public part, make her speech. Then the small talk that rises like wisps of fog will engulf her and drift up river with her, past Kenmore, past the westernmost suburbs of Brisbane, up into the Great Dividing Range. She will be able to make her escape. She is desperate for solitude and rainforest.

"Wonderfully done," someone enthuses, handing her another drink. "A fitting tribute."

She has skated through it then, on thin ice and champagne. Soon it will be possible to leave. She smiles and talks and laughs and talks and smiles. In her glass, the ice in the champagne punch twists and dwindles. She holds the glass up to the light. The icecubes are as thin as the wafers of capiz shell that wash up on Queensland beaches.

"Alison," someone says. "Congratulations. I just heard the news."

Alison holds herself very still. "Yes?" she says faintly. She will not be able to speak of it yet. They will have to excuse her.

"Your invitation to Sydney, I mean, for next year. You must be thrilled. When do you go?"

"Ah," she says. Her voice comes from a long way off. "Nothing can be done on a Sunday. I'll have to make arrangements in the morning."

Her colleague raises a quizzical eyebrow as she slides away, nodding, nodding, smiling. Discreetly heading for the cloakroom, head lowered, she collides with Walter who has propped himself against a shadowy window niche. She mumbles an apology and lurches on.

"Alison," he calls in his frail and elderly voice.

"Walter. Oh Walter, I'm sorry." She turns back and hugs him.

"Please join me," he begs.

"Oh Walter, I'm not fit company."

"You're my favourite company," he says. "These things, these things . . ." He waves vaguely at the room with his knobbed walking stick. "I find these things difficult. I only come because I'm perverse." Walter's own retirement party is twenty-five years behind him, though he has just recently published yet another scholarly book. "I'm the loneliest man in the world," he says. "Do you know how old I am?"

She knows of course, everyone knows, that he's ninety. The acuity of his mind and speech is a local wonder. Only time gets muddled for him. He gets the First and the Second World Wars confused; he fought in both.

"I'm as old as Methuselah," he says, "and as fond of Australians as ever. Have I told you why?"

He has of course. Many times. He has spoken of the Australian and New Zealand regiments stationed near his in Italy. That was during the Second World War. Or was it the first? In one of those wars, an Australian saved his life, dragging his wounded body through enemy fire.

"That was partly why," he says. "That was the beginning. But even more than that it's the whales."

"The whales?" she asks, politely. She has not heard about the whales.

"Dying on the beaches. All the way from Tasmania to Queensland, a shocking thing."

"When was this, Walter?"

"Now," he says, agitated, a little annoyed with her. "Here and now!" He is tapping on his forehead with his walking stick, a semaphore of distress. "Beached and gasping and dying by the hundreds."

"Walter, I hadn't . . ." She is confused. She is guilty of something. "I've heard nothing. Was this on the news?"

"Yes," he says. "And in the National Geographic. Stranded high and dry, out of their element, the loneliest, most awful . . ." There are tears in his eyes. "But the people of the coast are forming water lines, passing buckets, keeping them wet and alive. One by one, they are being dragged back to the water and towed out to sea. Wonderful people, the Australians. I walk along the beaches, you know, and watch. You hear a lot of rough talk out there, and some people think

Australians are crude, but I know what I see.''

He hunches into the window seat and stares out at the freezing lake. ''It was because of the whales that I sent my son out there, after the war. He never came back.''

''I didn't know you had a son in Australia, Walter.''

''School was never the place for him. It happens often, doesn't it, with the children of scholars? And after that trouble, after the penitentiary. I couldn't think of a better place to give him a fresh start. I thought: Australians will make a man of him. Look at the way they fight and the way they are with whales.''

''Walter,'' she murmurs, leaning her forehead momentarily against his. She is afraid of this confluence of griefs. She is afraid the sewer caps will not hold.

''What I'm sorry about,'' Walter says, ''is that I never told him . . . I mean, I should have said to him: I *am* proud of your racing car driving. There have been all these other things, all these . . . We go on and on, you know, fathers do, about the disappointments. But I should have told him: I do admire your courage and speed behind that wheel!''

In the window seat, he seems to fold himself up into nothing.

''I visited the place. I visit. I go there often, more and more often now. It's a very steep and winding road, you can see how dangerous. From Cairns up to the Atherton Tableland, do you know it?''

She nods, unable to speak. The roads of Queensland, north and south, are imprinted in her veins. She stares at the map of her forearm and sees the hairpin turns on the way from Cairns to Kuranda.

''You can see it was an accident, can't you?'' he says. ''He had everything to live for, a young wife and a little boy. We stay in touch. My grandson still sends me Christmas cards from Australia.''

"Sometimes," he says, "I think I may have told him I was proud of the driving. Sometimes I think I remember saying it."

"Walter,"'she says shakily, embracing him. "Merry Christmas, dear Walter. Forgive me. I have to go."

She manages, somehow to get out to her car. She sits in the darkness, holding herself very still. She turns on the car radio in time for the hourly news bulletin. "Sewer caps popping like corks," she hears. She turns it off and leans on the wheel and begins to shiver. She shivers violently, her teeth chattering, her body possessed by the shakes. Her bones clatter, even her skin is noisy, the din of her thoughts drowns out the tapping at her window. It is not until Walter leans across the front of her car and signals through the windshield that she can make him out, dimly, through the thin tough cataract of Sunday. She blinks several times. He taps on the window again.

"Walter," she says shocked, opening the door. "God, Walter, get in the car. You *mustn't* stand out in this cold, you'll catch your . . ."

"I would like to think so," he says quietly. "It's been a terribly long and lonely wait. Alison, you can tell an old man anything. What is it, dear child?"

"My mother," she begins to say. She puts her head against Walter's weathered shoulder and sobs. Orphaned at fifty: it sounds faintly embarrassing and comic, it's not supposed to be a major shock, it's not even listed in the register of traumas. "My mother," she begins again, quietly, "died in Brisbane at 4.40 a.m. this Monday morning."

She looks out at the frozen loop of a Queensland river. "My mother," she says, frowning a little, "died in the early hours of tomorrow morning."

Walter feels the car come plummeting off the Kuranda road, turning cartwheels through ferns and bougainvillea. It twists and twists and goes on falling through the gaping hole that opens somewhere behind his ribs. He hears the explosion that is now and always taking place.

"There is such gentleness," he says, stroking Alison's cheek, "in the most unexpected people, the roughest people. The way those men pass the buckets of water from hand to hand, the way they stroke the whales with wet cloths. I have never forgotten it."

Tomorrow, Alison thinks, I will fly all the way back to the beginning.